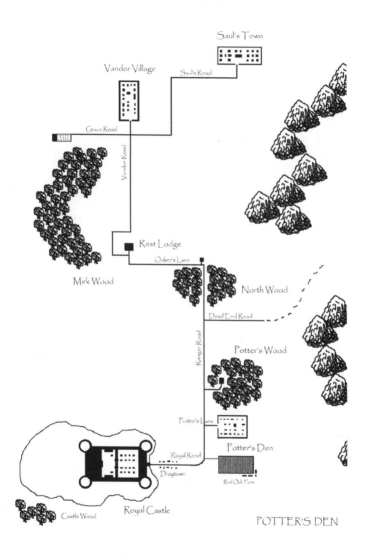

Soul's Town

Vandor Village

Soul's Road

Grove Road

Vandor Road

Rest Lodge

Oaker's Lane

Mirk Wood

North Wood

Dead End Road

Ranger Road

Potter's Wood

Potter's Lane

Potter's Den

Royal Road

Draytown

Red Oak Farm

Castle Wood

Royal Castle

POTTER'S DEN

The Seventh Tower

David Waghorn

authorHOUSE®

AuthorHouse™ UK Ltd.
500 Avebury Boulevard
Central Milton Keynes, MK9 2BE
www.authorhouse.co.uk
Phone: 08001974150

First published by AuthorHouse 9/19/2011

ISBN: 978-1-4567-7603-9 (sc)

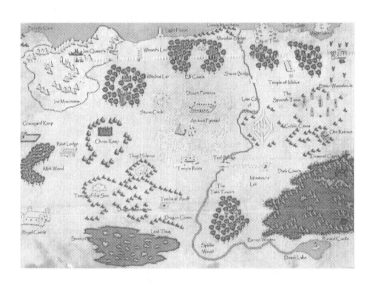

Chapter 1

My name is Samuel Furrowfield, I live in a small village called Potters Den. I work at a nearby farm called Red Oak Farm, feeding and cleaning the animals. My friends joke about the job that I have and think that I am stupid, and they all think that I can not get a better job. I could get a better job if I wanted to because I know a craftsman, but I usually answer my friends by saying at least I have money and a job that suits me.

My friends are John Beckly, Roger Forest, and Gillian Moredrake. After a hard days work we like to met up for a drink in the local tavern in Potters Den called The Dead Dog. John has been a friend to me since I was a boy, we used to play in the fields and woods together until it was dark. Our parents often told us not to play outside after dark as it was too dangerous at night because of woodland wolfs and orcs. I did not believe in orcs because I had never seen one and this made me want to stay out after dark just to try and get a glimpse of one to see if they really did exist, which got me in trouble with my parents and one time I was not allowed out for a whole month.

One day a group of orcs attacked our village hoping to steal whatever they could lay their hands on. That was the day I believed in orcs. I was just sixteen and that was when I first met Gillian. He was a wandering barbarian who had been staying at our village for the last four months. I had seen him before but never spoken to him let alone met him. Everyone treated him as an outsider and kept well away from him. My mother warned me to stay away from him but that made me more interested in him and I wanted to find out more about him. Gillian wore a brown leather waist coat with the shoulders badly cut. He had a black shoulder strap that went across his chest diagonally which held his long sword across his back. Gillian wore a black belt with a small bag attached to the side of the belt. He had a light brown leather animal skin tied around his waist. Gillian wore a head band and had a small medallion on a leather strap necklace around his neck. Gillian also wore barbarian boots made of leather straps and had animal hair at the top to keep water out.

On the day the orcs attacked the village he fought off the orcs killing about six of them before some of the orcs ran away. One of the orcs sneaked up behind Gillian while he was fighting and cut his side with it's sword. I threw a rock at the orc's head knocking him to the ground and Gillian turned to finish the orc off with his sword. I tried to run and tripped over a stone and the next thing I saw was Gillian reaching out his hand to pull me back up onto my feet. I took his hand and he said thank you for helping me with that orc. I became his friend after that and the village treated him as a hero after defending their village from the orc attack. The villages treated him like a royal guest for saving the village from the orc attack, so he decided to stay in our village. I mean who wouldn't if you got all your food and stay for free for the next four months. Gillian also taught me how to use a sword and I think I have become pretty good but not as good as Gillian, well not yet.

Roger Forest is a forest ranger, who helps hunters around the forest hunt for animals and helps them skin animals and teach them other forest skills. He also helps people get out of the forest if they got lost or get into danger. He is really skilled with a bow and a good hunter. If you ever get lost in a forest and Roger is with with you, you can be sure you will not go hungry. He does not drink much though. I guess it is because, he feels a sense of duty for his job.

Roger wore a dark green jacket with the flaps covering the tops of his legs. Roger had black leather shoulder pads and black leather wrist bands to protect his arm from the string of his bow when he used it. He had a black leather strap that went across his chest diagonally which carried his arrows on his back in a dark green arrow bag. Roger had light green trousers and wore, over the knee dark brown leather boots. Roger also had a bag strapped to the side of his belt that went round his waist.

John wore a brown jacket with flaps that covered the tops of his legs with dark brown shoulder pads. John wore a light brown shirt under his jacket and wore light brown trousers. John had a sword fixed to the side of his brown leather belt held in a sheath. On the other side of his belt he had a bag fixed to his belt. John wore dark brown leather boots with straps near the top of them. John also had a black leather shoulder strap that went diagonally across his chest but had nothing fixed to it, but a bag, or a quill of arrows, or a sword strap could be fixed to it if he needed.

I myself Samuel, wore a padded grey waist coat that covered the tops of my legs over a red shirt. I wore dark blue trousers and black leather boots. I had a bag fixed to a black leather belt, and on the other side I had a sword in a sheath fixed to my belt. We only carried our weapons with us if we needed them for hunting or sword practice.

My story begins when I was twenty years old. I was with my three friends in The Dead Dog tavern having a drink at a table near the right of the tavern close to the window, not too far away from the bar. When it was getting rather late about the tenth hour of the night judging by how high the moon was for that time of year during the months of spring, when all of a sudden we noticed a rather exhausted looking man enter the tavern. The man came straight towards our table holding a small bag in his hand and fell over our table and placed the bag into my hand and said; "Keep this safe for me."

I did as he said and hid the bag under my cloak jacket. The man then fell as if he was dead on the wooden floor of the tavern. At that moment four royal guards entered the tavern dressed in dark blue tunics, wearing silver breast plate armour, wearing red cloaks, silver helmets and leg guards. Two of the guards stood guard by the tavern entrance door. The other two looked around.

"Ere, looks like trouble", John said quietly to me.

On catching sight of the man on the floor by our table they rushed over to our table and started to search the man. The two guards then dragged him outside. I watched through the tavern window as they laid the man over one of their white horses and rode off with him in the direction of Castle Road which leads all the way to the Royal Castle. The two guards by the door went outside and stood guard outside as if to be waiting for someone else to come to the tavern.

"Hey what did that man give you?" John asked me.

"I don't know, but I do not like the look of all this. Don't tell anyone about what happened here tonight, any of you?" Samuel requested and got up to leave.

"Where are you going?" Roger asked.

"I better get out of here before those guards outside think I have anything to do with this", said Samuel and then headed towards the door to leave. Samuel walked past the guards and headed home.

When Samuel got home he lit a candle by his wooden desk and sat down on his wooden chair. He took out the bag the man gave him from under his cloak jacket. He emptied the contents of the bag onto his wooden desk. From the bag was a scroll tied by a single piece of string and a key with a label tied to it. On the label read: - Seven Oakers Lane, North Wood Cottage. Samuel thought to himself that you wouldn't write the address to your own house on a key unless you wanted to give it to someone to help them find the way to your house. Samuel thought if he knew where that address was and wasn't too sure. He untied the string and opened the scroll and it was a map. It was a map with all the land round about from the west where the Royal Castle was and their village and to the east The Seventh Tower which Samuel had only heard about in stories. To the north the City of Theb and to the south the dark Barren Wastes, which no man who had ever ventured too close to them had ever returned. The only men who had returned from that place had only seen the dark wastelands from the distance, or so Samuel had been told by others. Maybe it was to warn them away from such dreadful places. Samuel only knew a few places on the map such as the Royal Castle because it was not that far away from Potters Den and the city of Theb because it was a port for ships.

The next day Samuel took the bag with the map and the key with him and went to work as normal. When he returned home after he had finished his day's work he found his whole house searched and turned upside down. Samuel picked up his large back pack and put it onto his back. Feeling scared he went into the forest to look for his friend Roger who worked in the woods.

"Roger, I am glad you are still here", said Samuel.

"What is wrong, Samuel?" Roger asked.

"My house has been turned upside down", said Samuel.

"By whom?" Roger asked.

"I don't know, maybe those castle guards we saw last night", guessed Samuel.

"Has it got anything to do with what that man gave you last night?" Roger asked.

"I think so", answered Samuel.

"Did you know that man?" Roger asked.

"No, I have never seen that man before", answered Samuel.

"What did he give you?" Roger asked.

"He gave me a bag that contained a map and a key inside. The key has an address label on it", answered Samuel.

"Do you think you should hand it in to those guards?" Roger asked.

"I don't know, the man said to look after it for him", said Samuel.

"Maybe you should give the man back his bag", suggested Roger.

"How can I do that, the man has probably been taken to the castle dungeon by now", questioned Samuel.

"Well what are you going to do then?" Roger asked.

"Tell the others, Gillian and John to meet at your log cabin at ten tonight. I will hide there for a while", said Samuel.

"Okay then, I will tell them. I will go to Potters Den now and find them, and then I will meet you there at ten with the others", said Roger.

"Okay, see you then", said Samuel.

"Bye", said Roger.

The log cabin was built by Roger and he called it Rest Stop and it was in Potters Wood just north of Potters Den. All of Samuel's friends had been there many times. Many times they had stayed up late drinking and telling stories and playing cards.

At ten all of them met with Samuel and Roger at the log cabin.

"Samuel you are in a lot of trouble, the castle guards are looking for you. What have you done?" John asked.

"Nothing, but I think they after this map which that man gave to me last night. You know the one we saw in the tavern that got taken away by the kings guards", replied Samuel.

"Why is it so important to them?" Gillian asked.

"I don't know but I am going to find out", said Samuel.

"Shouldn't you just hand over the map to the guards and get yourself out of trouble?" John asked.

"Something is not right here, and I am going to find out what this is all about. We can find out more if we go to North Wood and find Seven Oakers Lane, this key has something to do with that address", said Samuel.

"Is this going to be dangerous?" John asked.

"Maybe, but I have wanted to do something daring like going on an adventure. Take a look at this map. It shows the whole valley and we could use this map to become adventures and search for gold and treasure", said Samuel.

"Don't you think you are dreaming a bit", said John.

"What else could this map be, I say we go to the address on the key and find out more. Maybe there will be more clues about this map at that address. Are you coming with me?" Samuel asked.

"Count me in, I haven't gone on any adventures for ages", replied Gillian.

"Well, you will need a good hunter for food and a good archer to protect you. You can count me in as well", said Roger.

"What about you John?" Samuel asked.

"I don't know, let me think about it and I will tell you in the morning", said John.

"If you go back without us John the guards will get suspicious and ask you where we went", said Samuel.

"Okay I will come with you, I could do with some holiday and adventuring", said John.

"John I need you to go back and get my sword from my house?" Gillian asked.

"Why me?" John questioned.

"Because you can sneak into my room without being seen by the guards. That is if they are still hanging around the village", said Gillian.

"Okay then, I will be back in an hour", said John.

"Oh, and John?" Samuel asked.

"What is it now?" John asked.

"Don't forget to bring some food back as well okay?" Samuel asked.

"Okay then", said John and then left the log cabin and headed back towards their village the Potters Den.

When John returned he showed them the food that he brought and gave Gillian his sword. They ate and afterwards they settled down for the night. They slept on the wooden floor of Roger's log cabin except for Roger who slept in his own bed.

"In the morning we will set off to find Seven Oakers Lane Cottage, but for now let's get some rest", said Samuel.

In the morning they ate eggs and bacon and bread. They all got ready for the journey ahead. Roger took his bow and case of arrows so he could hunt for food if need be. Gillian took his sword that John had brought from his home from Potters Den. They all set of early and Roger led them through North Wood until they found Seven Oakers Lane at the other side of the forest north of North Wood.

"Here is Seven Oakers Lane Cottage", said Roger.

"Well done Roger", said Samuel.

Samuel tried to open the door but it was locked. Samuel tried the key with the label on it but the key did not open the door.

"What are we going to do now?" John asked.

"We break in", said Samuel.

"Break in? That is against the law", said John.

"I need to find out what is going on", said Samuel.

"Oh well, I guess it's time to head back home", said John.

"I didn't come all this way for nothing and anyway the guards could already be looking for me", said Samuel.

"Well, you haven't done anything wrong, you could hand over this map to the guards and that would be the end of it", suggested John.

"John, aren't you even a little bit curious about what this map is about?" Samuel asked.

"Well, yes", replied John.

"I could break down the door for you", said Gillian.

"No, it's breaking the law", protested John.

"Look, the man who lived here has been taken by the guards. He gave me this map for safe keeping and he gave me this key with his address on it. He wanted me to come here, I need to find out what is going on and I believe I will find the answer inside", said Samuel.

"Okay, do what you want, but don't say to me later that I didn't warn you if the guards find out", warned John.

"Okay Gillian, break down the door", said Samuel.

Gillian rammed his shoulder into the door. The door buckled but didn't open. Gillian took a small run at the door and the door flung open breaking the lock.

"John stay outside and watch out just in case the guards come looking for us", said Samuel.

"All right", replied John and waited outside the cottage while the others took a look around inside.

"What are we looking for?" Roger asked.

"For a locked chest or something. That's what this key must be for", answered Samuel.

Samuel found a note on the table and read it to himself. It read : The royal guards have searched my house. I need to find a safe place to hid the map. Luckily I had the map on my person so they could not find it. I have tidied up the mess the royal guards left when they searched my house and I am now off to Potters Den to look for help.

In the Barren Wastes a demon lord lived in a dark castle that towered as high as the mountains that surrounded it. Lava pools covered the land and a stone bridge crossed a lava lake to reach his castle, but no man had ever seen it or dared venture that far into the Barren Wastes. By the demon lord's side was an undead wizard which served him. The demon lord sat at a black marble table with the undead wizard by his side. On the table was a crystal ball. The demon lord held his hands over the crystal ball until the mist inside the crystal ball cleared. As the mist inside the crystal ball cleared it revealed the face of a king.

"Where is the map oh king of Draytown?" The demon lord asked.

"My guards are out now searching for it. We have prisoner the man who had the map. We searched him and he didn't have the map on him. He must have given it to someone else before we captured him", replied the king.

"I don't want any secrets of the map to be discovered", said the demon lord.

"We will hunt down the map my lord", said the king.

"Do not fail me oh king, or I will send my orc armies to destroy your towns and villages", warned the demon lord.

"I will not fail you, I will have the map soon", said the king trembling.

"You better not, for your sake", said the demon lord and the mist covered the crystal ball again as it was before on his table.

Back at the cottage Samuel and his friends were searching through the cottage.

"I have found something interesting in the book shelf", said Roger.

"What have you found?" Samuel asked.

"It looks like a journal", replied Roger and opened the book. Samuel and Gillian gathered around the book as Roger opened it. "It looks like there are notes about the map and pictures of places and towers and ruins."

"Let me see?" Samuel asked. Samuel began to read at the front.

It read: There is a map that holds the key to find a precious magical sword. This sword is the key to defeating all enemies alive, undead or demonic. It is my quest to find this map and gather a band of fine brave men to help defeat the evil demon lord and his allies and free this land from evil...

Samuel flicked through the book a few pages and read again: ... I have searched many years and with the help of my friends and some brave, hired skilled men, I have found the map. I found the map hidden deep in the earth under the tomb of Azoff. I found a great former wizard buried there. I found him still grasping the map in his bony hand. We left the tomb after what I had searched for after so many years, taking all this time to find the map. As we left the tomb we headed towards the dragon mountains searching for a weapon to aid us on our quest. While we was near the dragon mountains all of a sudden we was attacked by a green fire dragon. The dragon breathed flames scorching the ground and devouring some of my men one after the other. Some of the other men were wounded and left for dead. Which I no doubt believe the green dragon would drag in his mouth to his dragon cave and eat for later. I hid in a nearby cave while the dragon was attacking my men hoping that the cave was empty of any monsters or dragons. Lucky for me the cave was empty. I waited until morning hidden in the cave and then fled back to my village alone as fast as I could at first light.

Once at home I studied the map. I discovered the key to where the magical sword was hidden which would help me defeat the demon lord. The Seventh Tower. It was guarded by the servant of the demon lord an undead wizard. The demon lord could not touch the sword for himself because it was forged by a battle wizard who had cast a spell on it to protect it against evil. The demon lord's servant the undead wizard froze the the sword in a block of ice and bound it in the very top of the highest tower so there it would be kept and protected so not to be a threat to his masters life.

The Seventh Tower has seven gates. Where Seven keys were hidden throughout the land. Each one of these keys can open each gate. Once with all these keys I can reach the seventh tower and gain the magical sword to kill the demon lord.

I have found this information from the libraries of the twin towers. The wizards keep a history of their past great wizards and catalogue a lot of knowledge of monsters surrounding these lands. They have many stories about races and the people that live in this land as well. Without this knowledge I would have been lost to even know where to search for these keys. This map which I have finally found will show me which place these keys have been hidden.

My next quest set me out to find each one of these keys which were hidden across this land. I have discovered the location of some of them and drawn pictures and notes about what lies in each guarded fortress that holds these keys. But for me as I gain trust of other men in trying to find these keys the news of me having the map spread to the dark demon lord himself and I have found myself battling against demons, and orcs, and ghosts of the undead as they have tried to get hold of the map and return it to their master. I know not what the road lies ahead for me.

Samuel closed the book.

"Well, what does it say?" Roger asked.

"It's a long story, but in short it talks about a powerful sword", replied Samuel.

"What I would do to get my hands on a powerful sword", said Gillian. "I sure could do with one of those."

"Well, let's all keep looking for this chest", said Samuel.

Roger searched inside the fireplace and found a lose stone and removed it. "I have it!"

The stone covered a hole which hid a long rectangular chest which was not very high. The chest was made of wood. Roger pulled out the chest and placed it on a table near the centre of the room. Samuel tried to use the key with the address label on it to unlock the chest and it unlocked the chest. Inside was a sword wrapped in a red cloth.

"Is this the sword the book was talking about?" Gillian asked.

"Let me have a look?", asked Samuel looking through the book and found a picture of the sword that Roger had found.

The journal read: … I have found a sword from the temple ruins in the desert. It has a magical crystal that warns of danger. It has saved my life many a time, for many monsters have tried to sneak up on me and it has warned me in times of need. The crystal in the base of the handle picks up the presence of all undead creatures and demons and starts to glow. I wait until I have found the true sword that is still locked away in the Seventh Tower.

"No, it is not the magical sword that the journal talks about of finding, but it is still a fine weapon", said Samuel.

"Are you finished in there yet?" John asked entering the cottage while Samuel held the sword. "Wow, what is that?"

"We found it in a chest hidden in the fireplace. The key the man gave me opened it", explained Samuel. "Can I keep it Roger?" Samuel asked Roger.

"I know I found it, but the man gave you the key and the map and I am best fighting with my bow and you have been trained with a sword", said Roger.

"Don't look at me, I have a sword and you need one", said Gillian.

"Okay it is mine then", said Samuel fixing it to his belt.

"What do we do know?" John asked.

"We get some rest somewhere and I will tell you more about the map", said Samuel.

"What, back to the village?" Gillian asked.

"No, it's too dangerous. Let's go to Rest Lodge, it's just a bit to the west from here and then we are there. I have a friend there too and he will help us out with a room for the night", said Samuel.

"To Rest Lodge it is then", said Roger.

They all travelled to Rest Lodge. They bought a drink each and some food and sat at a table near to a window on the right not so far from the bar. Samuel left their table to talk to his friend at the bar.

"Hello Bill", greeted Samuel.

"Hello Samuel. I haven't seen you for a while, how are things?" Bill asked.

"Not too bad", replied Samuel.

"Well, what can I do for you?" Bill asked.

"My friends and I need a room to stay in for a couple of nights?" Samuel asked.

"Sure, anything to help out an old friend. I have a room upstairs which sleeps four people. As long as there is no more than that?" Bill asked.

"Yes, that's fine. There is just the four of us", replied Samuel.

"Anything else?" Bill asked.

"Yes, can you take care of this for me for safe keeping during the night?" Samuel asked passing the map and his sword.

"Yea sure. I will keep it locked up in the cellar for you Samuel", said Bill.

Samuel and his friends spent most of the night drinking and then went up to the room Bill had let them use for the night.

In the morning Samuel looked around and noticed one of the beds empty. Samuel got up to wake the others.

"Gillian are you awake?" Samuel asked shaking him but all he got was a groan and he turned to the other side of the bed. "Roger, I think John has gone."

"Gone, gone where?" Roger said waking up with a start.

"I don't know", replied Samuel.

"Listen, I can hear horses coming this way", said Roger.

"Quick Gillian, get up!", said Samuel shaking Gillian.

"What's going on?" Gillian asked.

"John is missing and Roger can hear horses coming", explained Samuel.

Gillian got up and they all got dressed. Roger looked out of the window.

"It's the royal guard, they have found us, and John is with them", said Roger.

"What are we going to do?" Gillian asked.

"Well we can't escape horses on foot, so we best met with them and see if we can help John out", said Samuel.

The three of them went outside to met with the royal guards.

"Are you Samuel Furrowfield?" The guard asked.

"Yes I am, what do you want with me?" Samuel asked.

The guard then took out a scroll and read, "By order of the king, Samuel Furrowfield you are under arrest for stealing from the king."

"Stealing? Stealing what exactly?" Samuel asked.

"Take him away and his two friends back to the castle", said the guard.

"John, what is going on here?" Samuel asked.

"I am trying to protect you, just give them what they want and you will be free to go", said John.

"Give them what exactly?" Samuel asked.

"The map", whispered John.

They were all brought to the castle which was surrounded by a moat filled with water with a bridge that crossed over the moat towards the castle gate. On the way to the castle they passed a small group of houses which led up to the bridge of the castle. The houses around the royal castle was known as Draytown. The portcullis raised and they passed market stalls and a beggar in the centre of a open courtyard.

Samuel, Gillian and Roger had chains placed around their hands and brought in front of the king by six guards. The guards made them kneel before the king.

"Return what you have stolen from me and I will let you go free", said the king.

"I haven't stolen anything", said Samuel.

"The map, where is the map?" The king shouted at Samuel.

"Map, what map, I don't know what you are talking about?" Samuel said bravely.

"The map the man gave you in the tavern called the Dead Dog, I know he gave it to you", said the king angrily. "Don't lie to me, your friend John told me about the man that gave you a map, now where is it?" The king demanded.

"I must have lost it", said Samuel.

"Guards are you sure he doesn't have the map on his person?" The king asked.

"Yes sire, we searched him and his friends and they haven't got anything", replied the guard.

"Take them to the dungeon until I can think what to do with them. I have lost my patience with them", said the king.

"John, you will stay here, I have a few more questions for you", said the king.

"Yes, sire", replied John.

The guards took Gillian, Roger and Samuel to the dungeon and locked their legs in irons to the wall of the dungeon.

"John are you sure the man you saw taken prisoner by my guards gave the map to Samuel?" The king asked.

"Yes, he told me everything. I even saw the map for myself. And like you said, if I saw anyone with the map I should come and tell you, but I didn't even believe that such a map existed", said John.

"So where is the map now?" The king asked.

"I don't know sire, he must have hidden it somewhere and has not told me. I told you as soon as I could because I didn't want my friends to get into trouble", said John.

"You don't understand, until I have the map in my hand this kingdom is in great danger. If you find out where this map is let me know?" The king asked.

"Yes, I will sire", replied John.

"You may go now John to fed my horses stable boy", said the king.

"Yes, sire", replied John.

John hadn't been called stable boy for a while. He used to work for the king as a guard but had left a few years ago to search for a new job. He remembered when ever he had done something wrong as a punishment he had to clean out the kings horses.

"I can't believe John had us put into prison", said Gillian.

"Well, he did use to work for the king", said Samuel.

"Yea but not any more", said Gillian.

"Maybe he still has a sense of loyalty to the king", said Samuel.

"Why didn't you tell the king about the map?" Roger asked Samuel.

"That map that man gave me for a reason, and that map is the key to freeing this land from the evil demon who lives in the Barren Wastes", said Samuel.

"But if you tell the king where the map is we would all be set free", said Roger.

"Don't blame Samuel, it was John who told the king we had the map. Roger would you have told the king where the map was to put your friends in prison?" Gillian asked Roger.

"No, of course not, but I would tell him where the map is so we didn't have to stay in prison", said Roger.

"Look, it's no good arguing between us. If the worst comes to the worst I will tell the king where the map is hidden and we can all go free", said Samuel.

The king contacted the demon lord using his crystal ball in his personal chamber, "I summon thee oh great demon lord.

"What is it king?" Replied the demon lord.

"I have found the ones who have stolen the map and they are in my dungeon now", said the king.

"Have you the map?" The demon lord asked.

"No, they have hidden it somewhere and will not tell me where it is. My guards are searching Rest Lodge now as we speak", reported the king.

"If they do not tell you where it is kill them", said the demon lord.

The crystal ball clouded with mist and the image of the demon lord faded away.

John had sneaked into the kings chamber and had looked through the key hole and saw what the king was planning.

"The king is in league with a demon and he is going to kill my friends. What have I done?" John thought to himself.

John went to visit his friends in the dungeon. The guards let him alone with his friends.

"Well, look who it is, John the traitor", said Gillian.

"I came here to tell you something", said John.

"Well, maybe we are not interested", said Gillian.

"The kings going to kill you all in the morning", said John.

"What, why?" Roger asked shocked at the news as if being in prison wasn't bad enough.

"Just listen for a moment. The king is in league with a demon and he wants the map and he is going to kill you if you don't give it to him", said John.

"In league with a demon, are you sure?" Samuel asked in disbelieve.

"Shoosh! I am sure, I saw him talking to him using a crystal ball. I have to get you out of here", said John.

"Great, what are we waiting for", said Gillian.

"Wait, not now. There are too many guards in the castle. Wait until nightfall. I will come and get you", said John.

"We will be waiting here", joked Roger.

At midnight John came dressed in his old guard uniform and had his sword with him. John went into the dungeon and took the key from the guard who was asleep. He let his friends out and led them up the stairs from the dungeon.

"Wait here, I just need to check there are no guards ahead", said John.

"John, there are some guards coming up behind us, up this corridor. We will be discovered", warned Roger.

"Quick, hide in this room", said John.

They entered a room with four maidens trying on dresses and on seeing them one of them shouted, "Guards, come quick! Come quick, help!"

"Quick this way!" John said leading them down another set of stairs.

"I hope you know where you are going", said Gillian.

"Down here", said John holding open a wooden trap door in the floor.

John led them to a small boat and told them, "Climb in there, there is a boat just in front of you."

"I can't see a thing, why didn't you bring a torch with you John?" Roger asked.

"So the guards could not find us in the dark. Don't worry, I have worked everything out. Just hold onto the rope in the water and pull yourself along until we are out of the sewers", said John.

"I wondered what that strange smell was", said Gillian not knowing where they were.

They pulled on the rope until they came out from under the castle into the back of the castle moat. John used the oars inside the boat to reach the bank of the moat. They got out and John let the boat drift back into the water and then led them into the woods behind the castle.

"We are safe now", said John.

"That was some rescue plan John. Thanks for saving us", thanked Samuel.

"Well, when I found out what the king was up to I had to work out some kind of escape and I knew of the secret sewer entrance. And without any weapons to fight our way out and knowing how many guards were in the castle at night, I thought this was the safest way out", said John.

"So what happened to the map?" Gillian asked.

"I left it with my friend Bill at the tavern", answered Samuel.

"I guess it's back to Rest lodge then", said Roger.

"Yes", replied Samuel.

They went north through the forest and then over open grassy plains staying away from the roads so not to bump into any guards and draw attention to themselves. They reached Rest Lodge and knocked at the door.

Bill stuck his head outside his bedroom window, "What is it? It's the middle of the night. Oh is that you Samuel. Wait, I will be down in a minute to let you in."

Bill opened the door, "Welcome back my old friend. For a moment I thought the guards had caught you", welcomed Bill.

"Well they did, but thanks to John's change of heart he helped us escape", said Samuel.

"I'm glad to hear it. By the way those guards were asking about a map", said Bill.

"You didn't give it to them did you?" Samuel asked.

"No of course not. I got it hidden downstairs in one of the barrels. They searched the place but when they went down into the cellar all they saw was beer barrels. Follow me down here Samuel", said Bill grabbing a torch and led Samuel down the stairs into the dark cellar. Bill went towards the barrel and opened the lid and reached inside to give Samuel his sword and the map. "Here you go."

"Thanks Bill", thanked Samuel.

"No problem. You better find somewhere else to stay the night as the kings guards are looking for you and they know you have stayed here", said Bill.

"Bill, do you know anywhere where we can get some money?" Samuel asked Bill.

"Well I don't have any I can lend you and it would take you a while to earn some working in my tavern, but I have heard about some buried treasure", said Bill.

"Go on", said Samuel.

"I had some sailors in here once or I should say pirates just a little while back. They were bragging about raiding a ship which was carrying the king's gold from the port of Theb. The pirates knew the royal guards would search their homes looking for the stolen gold so they hid it in a cave. The royal guards did search the pirates homes and found nothing of the stolen king's gold. I heard one of them say they hid it in a place called Pirates Cove", said Bill.

"Any idea where that is?" Samuel asked.

"No, I have never heard of it, and I don't suppose that any of those pirates are going to tell you if you ever got hold of one", said Bill.

"Oh well", said Samuel.

"Sorry I can't help more but I can offer you this wooden shield. I have had it all these years hanging up above the bar and never truly needed it. If you're, going after pirates and their treasure this shield could come in handy for protection", said Bill.

"Thanks", thanked Samuel.

"Oh and here are your friends weapons. I locked them down in the cellar as well for safe keeping like", said Bill.

"Oh Bill, do you think there is any chance that the pirates treasure is still hidden there in this so called cave?" Samuel asked.

"Yes, because I heard one of the pirates say, if it wasn't for a band of frogmen that had made camp in that cave that they would be able to get their hands on that there gold. If you want to find out more head north to the next village called Vandor", suggested Bill.

"Bill is it okay if me and my friends can stay just for one more night?" Samuel asked.

"Well I think it would be best if you head straight to Vandor or the kings guards might come looking for you again", said Bill.

"Yes, you are probably right", said Samuel.

Samuel and his friends left the tavern and went outside. They camped in Mirk Wood for the rest of the night to try avoid the royal guards finding them. Soon it was morning and John cooked them breakfast on the fire. He made them rabbit stew.

"Where now?" John asked.

"We head north to the village of Vandor to find somewhere to stay", said Samuel.

"Why not stay at Rest Lodge with Bill for free?" Gillian asked.

"It's too dangerous. Once the kings guards come after us, that will be the first place they look", said Samuel.

"I will stand guard all night and be ready for them this time", said Gillian.

"That is very brave of you Gillian but I don't think even you can fight all of the kings royal guards by yourself. It will be safer to move on", said Samuel.

Samuel and his friends headed towards the village of Vandor following the road north from Rest Lodge. They arrived after travelling for two hours and entered the tavern called the Red Lion.

"Inn keeper, can we have a room for four people to stay the night please?" Samuel asked.

"I see you are travelling with one of the kings guards. You can come in and take rest in one of our rooms" said the inn keeper.

"How much will it cost?" Roger asked.

"Usually it costs 60 gold crowns but for you 40", said the inn keeper.

Roger paid the inn keeper with money he brought with him from home. They bought some food from the tavern and some drinks. They stayed in the tavern the rest of the day and when it was night time the inn keeper showed them to their room. The inn keeper led them down some stairs to their room. They all took a bed each which had old grey sheets and they could see the scurry of mice under the beds.

"40 gold crowns for this!" Gillian commented after seeing the room.

"It would have cost us more if I didn't have my royal guards uniform on", said John.

"Well let's get some rest for tomorrow", said Samuel.

Everyone got into their beds and rested down for the night.

"Tell Samuel, why did you come here?" Roger asked.

"Well we need some money to by weapons and armour before we go on the quest for the magical sword, and Bill told me about a treasure of stolen gold hidden in pirates cove. I have studied the map and found where pirates cove is. Bill said I could find out more in this village. I have also read the journal and it said that pirates cove has been used for smuggling by pirates for years but it is not known to everyone. It is a pirates secret the journal says, and it also says he found out from a pirate when he asked him if he knew about the cave near the seashore and the pirate said that he better keep clear of that cave because pirates use it for smuggling and if anyone went near the cave they would be hunted down by the pirates", explained Samuel.

"And is there anything guarding this treasure?" John asked.

"Just a band of frogmen, but they will be no match for us, especially with Gillian with us", replied Samuel.

The next morning Samuel woke up and went outside for some fresh air. The room they were staying in was stuffy in the basement. He saw outside four gallows with four dead men hanging on them. One wore an expensive looking coat and another wore breeches like a sailor.

Samuel saw a man walking by and asked, "Who were these men?"

"They were pirates who were hiding in the village from the kings guards. They were accused of stealing the king's gold and were hanged here. But the guards never found where the pirates hid the treasure", answered the man.

John came rushing out of the tavern, "Oh thank goodness you are okay. I thought when I saw you gone that the kings guards had captured you."

"I just went out to get some fresh air", said Samuel.

"Take a look at this", said John handing Samuel a poster.

Samuel unrolled the poster and saw it was a sketch of himself and it read: Wanted, reward 80 gold crowns.

"Get the others, we have to get going right away", said Samuel.

Chapter 2- The First Quest

The four of them travelled north following the map to the pirates cave. They pass the graveyard keep and travelled over green hills and travelled north near the mountains. They kept the mountains in sight to their right as they travelled over green hills until they finally reached a small group of mountains. As they reached the final mountain near the seashore they found an opening in a cliff by the beach. As they entered there were torches lit along the cave wall which led down a corridor until it came to a junction that went left and right.

"Which way do we go now Samuel?" John asked.

"Roger, check for any traps", said Samuel.

"I found a trap to the right", said Roger.

"Then we shall take the safer route to the left", said Samuel.

As they followed the cave left it twisted round and went up. A frogman was standing on guard and had his sword in it's hand ready to fight. The frogman had big yellow frog like eyes and green scaly skin and had a head like a frog but a body shaped like a human. It wore a blue cloth round it's waist and a belt across it's shoulder with a bag fixed to the belt on it's back.

"Leave this to me", said Gillian eager for battle.

Gillian had his sword raised ready to strike and with one overhead blow from his sword killed the frogman. Gillian searched the dead frogman for anything useful and found 10 gold crowns in it's bag.

"Look, this must be part of the pirates treasure", said Gillian.

"Least we are in the right place then", said Samuel.

"On to the treasure then", said John excited with the thought of finding more gold.

"Wait, not so fast!" Warned Roger grabbing hold of John.

"What's the matter? You want all the treasure for yourself?" John asked.

"No it's not that, it's something else. Something is not quite right", said Roger.

Roger slowly edged to the wall and found a trip wire.

"Have you found something Roger?" Samuel asked.

"Yes, it looks like a trip wire for a trap. Keep moving slowly along this side of the wall", warned Roger.

Once past the trap the floor changed and became more refined like stone floor tiles and then further ahead they came to a door. Roger opened the door with his bow aimed ready and saw another frogman inside the room. Roger fired killing the frogman before it got a chance to attack.

"It's safe now, you can all come in", said Roger.

The rest of them entered the room and saw the dead frogman on the floor.

"Nice work Roger", said Gillian.

Roger searched the body and found another 10 gold crowns. "Here's more of that gold."

Gillian noticed something on a table in the room, "What's this?" Gillian asked picking up a green herb from the table.

"It's a herb for healing small wounds. I have seen this type before in the forest", answered Roger.

Gillian put the herb into a small pouch on the side of his belt. They found nothing else useful in the room and left the room by another door to continue down the corridor. They came to another junction that went left and right. They went left and found another room.

"My turn to kill what is on the other side of that door", said John.

John readied his sword and rushed in with his sword raised.

"Be careful", said Samuel.

John let out a scream and Roger came to his aid and grabbed him holding his cloak stopping him from falling forward any further. John had rushed into a room with a pit in the middle full of snakes and almost fell in, if it wasn't for Roger grabbing hold of him in time.

"Thanks again Roger", thanked John.

"Now that's two you owe me", joked Roger.

"What's happening?" Samuel asked. From outside the room standing next to Gillian.

"It's a pit trap full of snakes. You both better stay outside, there is not much room to move in here", said Roger.

"All right then", said Samuel.

"Look a chest on the other side of the room", said John pointing to it greedily.

"Stay here while I try to reach it", said Roger.

Roger walked around the outside of the room with his back against the wall, edging his feet slowly around the edge of the pit. John watched with baited breath while Roger edged his way around the room. Roger got to the back wall near where the chest was and was almost within arms reach from the chest. He leaned forward towards the chest and his foot started to slip. Roger stood back to take a breath and then tried again. He reached out with one arm and then the other and grabbed the chest firmly with both hands. Roger then edged back the way he came until he reached the door and got back into the corridor again and breathed a huge sigh of relief. Roger opened the chest and found 50 gold crowns inside and shared them with the others in their group.

They headed back into the corridor the way they came and took the right path. Frogs began to jump along the path and one bit into the side of Samuel's leg. Samuel let out an ouch and Gillian made short work of the frogs by killing them. The path twisted north and then east again until they came to a small portcullis which was lowered blocking their path. Gillian tried to lift it and then John and Samuel joined in to help lift it.

"It's no use, it is too heavy", said Samuel.

"Come over here, I have found a hidden door", said Roger.

As Roger entered the hidden room two frogmen attacked him catching him by surprise and one cut his arm. Samuel came in and fought one and killed it, while Gillian rushed in to kill the other one. They searched the frogmen and found 10 gold from each one.

"Everyone search the room", said Roger.

"But it's empty", said John.

"Just keep searching", said Roger.

"What are we searching for exactly?" John asked.

"A hidden switch or a leaver or something", answered Roger.

Samuel stood on a slightly raised stone and it sunk into the floor.

"Oh, I hope that wasn't another trap", said Samuel.

The clanking sound of an iron gate was heard in the corridor. They returned to the corridor to see the portcullis raised so they could continue up the corridor. They passed under the open portcullis gate and came to a set of stairs leading down into a lower level.

The four of them walked along a new corridor until they came to a door. Samuel opened the door slowly and took a look inside the room. The room was large and there was a small wooden chest on the floor at the other end of the room. The others enter the room behind Samuel.

"Look a chest!" John exclaimed.

"No, wait!" Roger said.

"Why, there is nothing to stop us, no frogmen monsters, nothing", said John.

"Okay, let's all move slowly to the chest together", said Samuel.

As they passed the centre of the room their feet pushed down on some lose floor tiles and made a noise.

"What was that?" Gillian asked.

"Another trap maybe?" John guessed.

"Quick, run!" Samuel shouted as part of the ceiling started to fall down behind them.

"Is everyone all right?" Samuel asked.

"Yes", came the reply from the others.

"The rumble from the ceiling has blocked off the door and we can not get out", said Samuel.

"I will look for a secret door", said Roger.

"I hope this chest was worth it", said Samuel.

John opened the chest and found a purple bottle inside.

"Should I drink it?" John asked.

"I don't know", said Samuel.

"I have found a secret door, come this way", said Roger.

"John, take the bottle with you", said Samuel.

John was getting thirsty so took a quick sip of the liquid from the bottle. He started to cough and splutter.

"Are you all right John?" Samuel asked.

"Yes fine, but it didn't taste so good", replied John.

The secret door led them to the previous corridor and they continued following it round to the right until they came across a pool. Gillian started to cross the pool and a piranha fish bit his ankle and he yelled out in pain and jumped out of the pool of water onto the other side.

"Be careful, those fish are dangerous", warned Gillian.

"Samuel, I don't feel too good", said John. Sweat was dripping down the side of John's face and he was shaking like he had a fever.

"It has to be that bottle he took a drink from, it's poison", said Roger.

Samuel took the bottle and was about to throw it on the floor when Roger stopped him.

"Wait, we can use this to cross the pools", said Roger.

Roger took the poison and poured it into the pool full of piranha fish. The fish started to die and float up to the surface.

"It should be safe to cross now", said Roger.

They came to a path which went left and right. Roger searched for traps.

"I found another trap on the left", said Roger.

"This place is full of traps", said Gillian.

"The pirates protected that treasure of their's well", said Samuel.

They took the right path to avoid the trap and a green blob dropped from the ceiling and Gillian reacted slicing his sword through it with ease. They came to another door and entered the room. A frogman stood guard ready for them. Samuel attacked the frogman and after a few attacks killed the monster. There was a cupboard in the room and Samuel searched the cupboard and found a gold looking jug with the words "Anti-poison", written on it.

"John, take a drink of this", said Samuel.

John took the jug and drunk slowly. John started to feel better and the fever left him. They left the room and returned to the corridor. They continued down the corridor until they came to a small pool of water with a fresh stream running into it.

Samuel took a drink, "Come drink, it's refreshing.

All of them took a drink from the pool.

"I feel stronger", said Gillian and his ankle started to heal.

They continued until they reached another door and opened it. Bats flew out and John and Samuel fought them off with their swords. They entered the room and John trod on a lose floor tile.

"I hope that wasn't another trap", said John.

Roger found a cord running along the wall, "It looks like that switched triggered something in another room."

They left the room and followed Roger into the next room. A stone bridge had been lowered across a chasm in the middle of the room. On the other side of the bridge was a chest. A blob fell from the ceiling and Roger took aim with his bow and killed it. Roger crossed the bridge and opened the chest.

"It's gold, about 50 gold crowns", said Roger.

"Well done Roger", said Samuel.

"That switch must have lowered the stone bridge across the chasm", said Roger.

They left the room in search for more treasure. They came to a dead end.

"What now?" Gillian asked.

"There has to be more gold than this", said John.

A stone door opened and two frogmen guards came out. John and Gillian fought them both and Samuel went inside the room and fought with another frogman inside. They took 30 gold from the dead frogmen and found another chest inside the room. It contained 100 gold crowns.

"We did it, we found the pirates treasure!" Exclaimed Samuel.

They collected the gold and exited out the cave the same way they came in watching out for the traps they had found on the way in.

"Where do we go now?" John asked.

"Well the kings guards will be looking for us in Vandor so I think we should head to the next village", replied Samuel.

They moved on and headed east until they came to a small town which was called Saul's Town. They rested in a tavern called the Sly Fox, and the next morning they celebrated with a drink. The tavern cost them 60 gold crowns to stay in. They heard stories of goblins burning homes and stealing gold and swords from their town. Then they left the tavern and visited the towns blacksmith.

"What can I do for you?" The blacksmith asked.

"We need some armour", said Samuel.

"Armour I have, swords I don't. I still have many to make to defend our town from wretched goblins. From their last attack they stole our swords so I don't have any swords to sell you", said the blacksmith.

"Do you have any chain mail?" Samuel asked.

"Yes, here you go, that chain mail there costs 80 gold crowns", replied the blacksmith.

"Do you have any leather armour?" Gillian asked.

"Yes, for 10 gold crowns", answered the blacksmith. "Now is there anything else you want?"

"Do you have a small shield?" John asked.

"Yes, this one is 80 gold crowns", said the blacksmith.

They bought the shield and armour. Gillian wore the leather armour, John took the small shield and Samuel put on the chain mail armour.

As they went back to the tavern a man with a chain round his neck stopped them.

"Wait, you warriors our town needs your help", said the man.

"Who are you?" John asked.

"I am governor over this town. I need your help. Goblins have been attacking our town month after month and we have lost good men to these Goblins and we have lost homes and gold and weapons. I fear if they attack again soon we will not be strong enough to defend ourselves", said the governor.

"What do we get in return?" Samuel asked.

"You can have this gold chain as a reward. It's worth a 100 gold crowns. It's all I have left which I managed to hide from them", said the governor.

"Where are these goblins found?" Samuel asked.

"If you look towards those mountains you will find a cave. The goblins are at the cave. Find and kill the goblin leader and bring back his head and shield as prove and I will give you this chain as a reward", said the governor.

"We will help you, we will rest tonight and we will search out this goblin leader in the morning", said Samuel.

"Thank you so much. I will make sure the tavern keeper will not charge you for your stay here. Thanks again, our town is very grateful to you all", said the governor.

Samuel and his men bought some food suppliers and some sheep skin blankets for the journey ahead. Their journey took them south and then east below the desert. They headed towards the river and headed east where a large stone bridge was. A man of older years but not exactly old sat near the sign which directed the way towards Troll Bridge to the east, north to Stone Bridge and the City of Theb.

"Are you travellers heading towards the City of Theb?" The man asked.

"No, we are heading towards the mountains on the other side of the river", Samuel replied. "Why do you ask?"

"It is just that if you are thinking of taking a sort cut by going over Troll Bridge, I would warn against it. A large troll guards the bridge and only lets goblins and orcs across it. Some say he is in league with the demon lord who lives in the Barren Wastes. Any traveller who has tried to cross it has been killed. Just the other week I heard a merchant with his wagon tried to cross Troll Bridge and the troll threw his wagon into the river and chased the man to kill him. The man jumped over the side of Stone Bridge and swam to the bank and then fled back the way he came. Lucky for him trolls are not too fast and can not swim", warned the man.

"Thanks for the warning. Is there another way across the river?" Samuel asked.

"Yes, if you head north and follow the path and then go over Stone Bridge, you will be a lot safer", suggested the man.

"Thank you", said Samuel.

"Your welcome", said the man.

They followed the path north towards Stone Bridge. The bridge was made of grey stone and was wide enough for a wagon to cross. It took them a days journey to reach the other side of the river from Saul's Town. The next day they planned to travel south towards the mountain where the goblin cave was.

"It's starting to get dark now. I think its time to set up camp and get some rest for the battle against the goblins tomorrow", said Samuel.

Roger gathered sticks to make a fire. Gillian made camp using some tree logs covered by animal skin. They sat around the fire and cooked their food which they had brought from Saul's Town. After they had eaten they put the fire out and slept under their sheep skin blankets that they had also bought from Saul's Town.

The next day after they had ate again they readied their weapons and armour for the journey south towards the mountains, leaving their camp as it was. As they neared the mountains they saw two goblins standing guard. Gillian raised his sword and charged towards them ready for battle. The two goblin guards ran towards their goblin cave entrance to warn the goblin band. Samuel, John and Roger all started to run to catch up with the goblins.

"Roger, shoot them before they are alerted of our presence!" Samuel ordered.

Roger took aim killing one of them hitting the goblin in the back. The other panicked quickly cumbering over rocks towards the entrance cave. The goblin was too quick for them and easily out ran them as he climbed over the rocks, but Gillian was gaining slowly on him and the goblin knew soon there would be no escape for him. The goblin stopped and took from his belt a horn and held it ready to blow it to warn his band of danger. Gillian still wasn't close enough to stop him. Roger took aim and fired another arrow killing the goblin before he could blow his horn.

"That was close", said John.

Roger took the horn from the goblin and Gillian took 10 gold crowns from each of the goblin's pockets which were on their belts.

The goblin had led them to the cave entrance and they entered slowly. Samuel led from the front and took a torch from the wall to see down the cave. The cave was dark except for some touches fixed to the walls of the cave. They came to a junction and headed left. A bat flew towards Samuel and scratched his shoulder with its small claws. Gillian took one swing with his sword and killed it. The passage turned right and there was a door on either side. They first entered the door to their right which led into a small room. A chasm blocked their way to a door on the other side, and there was a bridge which was raised in the air on the other side of the chasm. There were also two snakes crawling around on the other side.

"How are we going to get across?" John asked.

"We need to find a switch to lower that bridge", suggested Roger.

They left the room and entered the door on the left. Two goblins were inside and raised their swords ready to fight. John and Gillian took a goblin each. The goblin that John fought was quite skilled and John used his shield to defend against the goblins blows. John soon learnt the goblin's technique and as the goblin swung his sword for a head blow at him, John raised his shield to defend against the attack and thrust his sword into the goblin's chest. Gillian was quite skilled in combat and killed the goblin he was fighting after three attacks. They search the goblins and took 10 gold crowns from each and saw in the room a weapons rack. Roger searched the rack and found some arrows and a wooden shield.

"Samuel, you could use this shield. I know it's not much but it's better than nothing", said Roger.

"Well this wooden shield I got from Bill was quite old and I think it got damp from the pirates cave. I think I could do with a new one. Thank you", said Samuel taking the wooden shield and fixed the strap to his arm. They left the room through a door on the other side of the room and entered a passageway. Another bat flew towards them. Roger took aim and killed it with an arrow. They continued along the passage and the passageway turned to the right again. Samuel scanned the passage with the torch and saw a door ahead built into the left wall, there was also a bat hanging from the cave ceiling. Roger took aim and fired knocking the bat dead to the ground. They entered the door on the left wall and Gillian entered with his sword ready. A goblin stood guard ready for attack. Gillian killed him with a few strokes of his sword. Gillian took 10 gold crowns and the others entered the room. There was a wooden wheel with rope leading from it into the ceiling.

"This must be the switch to lower the bridge in the other room", said Samuel.

Gillian turned the wheel until the rope went tight, then they headed back to the room with the chasm blocking the room. As they entered, the bridge was already lowered and they crossed over watching the two snakes carefully. The snakes reared up at John and he attacked them, slicing them both in half one after the other. They opened the door carefully expecting more goblins inside. Gillian went first.

"All clear, no goblins", replied Gillian.

There was a cupboard on the left wall of the room and a chest at the far end of the room. Samuel walked towards the chest and a dart from the wall fired out hitting Samuel in the arm. As Samuel still moved on another dart fired from the wall.

"Watch out!" John shouted.

Samuel used his shield to defend himself and the dart stuck into his shield.

"Come back Samuel, it looks like a trap", said John.

Samuel moved back slowly and Roger examined his arm.

"Is it bad?" Samuel asked.

Roger pulled the dart from his arm and examined it. "It looks like it was tipped with poison."

"Maybe the anti-poison is in the chest?" Gillian said.

"Or in the cupboard", said John and started to search the cupboard. John found a lever and puled it.

"I think I just switched the trap off."

Gillian walked slowly towards the chest and opened it. Inside was 20 gold crowns. "No anti-poison, but their was some gold though. 20 gold crowns."

They continued on to look for any anti-poison to help Samuel. They came to another junction and Roger searched for traps and then they turned right.

"It's a dead end ", said Gillian.

John took a rest for a while and leaned against the wall. The wall started to move back under John's weight. "I think I have found a secret room."

They entered a room where there was a pool of water. They all drunk from the pool after Roger said that it was fresh enough to drink.

I feel a lot better now", said Samuel after drinking the water.

"It must have an anti-poison in it", said John.

They continued on and took the left passage which led them to a passage that turned right. A claw claver leapt from the darkness and attacked Gilian. John leapt to Gillians aid and defended himself from the cave claver's claws with his shield. A cave claver was a brown monster with long teeth and long claws and had eyes that could see in the dark. John killed the monster with a blow to it's chest and it fell lifeless to the floor. Just ahead were some stairs that led down to another cave level. They all went down the stairs to the lower level.

As they walked along the passage it turned right. Another bat attacked them and John killed it with an overhead swing of his sword. They entered a room on the right wall and it was so dark they could not see inside. Samuel used his torch to see near the wall and revealed a red key hanging on a black metal hook fixed to the wall. Samuel takes the key and they continue on. They come to a junction and Roger searches for traps and he finds a pit trap in the floor.

"Be careful ahead, there is a pit trap", said Roger.

"Does this mean we are near the goblin leader?" Samuel asked.

"It must be to stop anyone from entering their lair", replied John.

"We must jump over the pit", said Roger.

"Is there any other way?" Samuel asked.

"No, this is the only way", answered Roger.

Samuel took a run up and jumped over the pit. Gillian took a run and jumped the pit next. Then Roger jumped and cleared the pit trap. John took his armour off and threw it over to Samuel so he wouldn't be slowed down when he took a run up. John started to jump the pit and started to lose his balance. Samuel grabbed his hand to save him.

"Thanks", thanked John.

"No problem", said Samuel.

They continued to go down the passage and goblins came from passages either side to attack them.

"Take your positions", warned Samuel.

They fought each goblin as it attacked, killing them one by one. After the goblins were killed they entered the lair of the goblin leader.

There were tables and chairs in the room. On the table were attack plans that the goblins were planning. Two goblins guarded their leader. Their goblin leader wore a wooden shield with a black goblin face painted on it.

"Gillian and John, take those guards and I will take the goblin leader", ordered Samuel.

The goblin leader growled and stood up to attack Samuel fixing his shield to his arm. The goblin leader defended against Samuels blows well and Samuel defended against the goblins blows. The battle was even between them, no one person better than the other. Samuel pushed the goblin leader back with his foot then Roger took aim and fired an arrow at the goblin leader. The arrow stuck into the goblin leader's shield. Samuel and the goblin leader continued to fight. Samuel beat against the goblins leader's sword again and again, and then took a lunge at the goblin leader killing him in the chest. Gillian and John had killed the goblin leader's guards. Samuel swiped off the head of the goblin leader and put it into a sack and took the goblin leader's shield as prove for the governor of Saul's Town. A red door was at the back of the room. Samuel used the red key he had recently found to open the door. Samuel entered the small room which contained a small chest containing 100 gold crowns. Samuel took the treasure while his men searched the dead goblins for more gold and they found another 40 gold. Then they left the goblin caves full of cheer after completing yet another successful quest and made their way back to their camp for the night to eat and get some rest.

They headed back to Saul's Town the next day and were greeted by grateful towns folk. The governor of the town also greeted them. Samuel showed the governor the goblin's shield and the goblin's head.

"You have done well and you have saved our village from the goblins. Our village can have peace again. As promised here is my governor's chain", said the governor handing over his chain to Samuel.

Samuel took the chain, "Thank You."

The chain had a purple stone in the centre. Samuel put the chain around his neck.

"Why don't you stay a while?" The governor offered.

"Okay then, but only for a few days then, my men deserve a rest", said Samuel.

Roger whispered in Samuel's ear, "Is that wise to stay when the kings guards are searching for us?"

"We need to find out where the next quest treasure is to help us on our quest", replied Samuel.

"Okay then, but only for a few days then", agreed Roger.

The next day Samuel asked some people in the town if they knew any stories about any ancient treasures. He found a person who knew of a tomb where a great wizard was buried.

The man told the story:-

"In Graveyard Keep there is a tomb. There is buried a great wizard which is said that he had a magical armour that even wizards themselves could use. Hidden underground are passages which lead to the wizard's tomb. Many say it is haunted by ghosts and zombies. They say the wizard cursed the tomb with the undead to protect him and his treasure. Only the brave can venture into this tomb. Many warriors have either died trying to find the wizards treasure or run out screaming in fear", said the man.

"I don't like ghosts or zombies. It sounds scary", said Gillian.

"I'm not scared", said John.

"We will try and find this treasure", said Samuel.

"I thought you would say that", said Gillian.

The next day a man rode into Saul's Town and gave a message to the governor. The message was from the king of Draytown. The governor read the message to himself. It read:

From the king of Draytown.

To the Governor of Saul's Town.

I have heard of the heroic deeds of the company of men which I believe are staying in your town of Saul's Town. These men are wanted by the king for high treason against the king. We request you to hand over these wanted men or we will be forced to enter your village and take them from you by force. If you hide these men from us, your village will be put under our guard and your tax doubled for the following five years.

From the king of Draytown.

"Samuel, may I speak with you?" The governor asked.

"Yes of course, what is it?" Samuel asked.

"You are in danger. The king of Draytown is on his way here to capture you and your men", said the governor.

"How did he find out?" Samuel asked.

"Your fame for saving our town must have spread to other nearby villages. I'm sorry, I can not protect you or my town will be in danger from the king", explained the governor.

"I understand", said Samuel.

"It would be best for you and your men to leave now", said the governor.

"Yes, I will gather my men and be gone", said Samuel.

Samuel bought some food supplies and gathered his men together and headed west towards Graveyard Keep.

"Samuel, where are we heading?" John asked.

"To Graveyard Keep for the next quest", replied Samuel.

"But what if the kings guards pass us while we are travelling that way?" John asked.

"Not if we go through the mountains", said Samuel.

Samuel led his men through the mountain path between two sets of mountains on either side.

"Isn't this where bandits wait for weary travellers?" John asked Roger.

"Yes, and I guess this is why this is the safer route to avoid the kings men", said Roger.

All of a sudden arrows flew from the air over their heads, one or two at a time.

"Take cover, it's a bandits ambush", said Roger.

They took cover behind some rocks. Bandits came running down the side of the mountain on both sides. Roger took aim and fired killing two of them. The bandits wore animal skins and carried axes. Gillian attacked one of the bandits cutting his arm off as he raised his axe. Gillian took the axe and threw it killing another bandit. Six more bandits surrounded them. Roger fired killing another one with his bow. Samuel and John took positions to fight them. They killed three more between them and the other two fled back into the mountains. Gillian picked up one of the bandits throwing axe to keep as a weapon for himself.

They continued their journey until they reached Mirk Wood and set up camp for the night.

The next morning after they had eaten they moved through the cover of Mirk Wood north towards Graveyard Keep. They discovered an old looking hut with a man standing outside dressed in a blue shiny cloak.

"Good morning to you, and what brings you through this wood?" The man asked.

"We are on our way to Graveyard Keep", replied Samuel.

"Are you grave robbers?" The man asked.

"We are of sorts, we are looking for a treasure left by a great wizard said to be in the tombs of Graveyard Keep", replied Roger.

"I have heard of the legend as well but no one has ever succeeded in finding the treasure and survived the tomb. They say it was cursed by the wizard himself to protect the treasure", said the man.

"That is what we have be told as well. So the stories are true then?" Samuel asked.

"I guess so, but I don't know for myself", said the man.

"So you know a lot about this tomb?" Samuel asked.

"I have heard many stories from my master. My name is Elrond. I am a young wizard. My master taught me to be a wizard, and in his old age he left to find peace and quiet during his old age", explained Elrond.

"Can you help us, you seem to know more than us about this tomb?" Samuel asked.

"Well, I have only heard stories, but my magic could be some help to you and I guess there is nothing for me here any more since my master left. I will join you on your quest", said Elrond.

"Thank you very much", thanked Samuel.

"What is that around your neck?" Elrond asked.

"It was given to me as a reward for helping the governor of Saul's Town", replied Samuel.

"That is no ordinary chain. That is an amulet. And if I am right an amulet of courage. You will need that if you are to brave undead monsters which lay in wait inside the graveyard keep", said Elrond.

"I am not scared", said Samuel boldly.

"May I have it then?" Gillian asked.

"Yes, take it Gillian and I hope it will give you courage against undead monsters", said Samuel.

"Why are you so scared of ghosts and zombies Gillian. I have never seen one before and I don't even know whether I believe in them or not", said John.

"Believe me, they exist all right. I use to think they didn't exist until one evening as a youngster I was near the dead woods near my lands and it was misty and I saw three ghosts hovering above the ground. They had white tattered clothes and skull faces and bony arms. And their eyes where red as if chanted by some kind of evil magic", explained Gillian.

"Let me get my things and I will join you, come inside for a while", said Elrond.

Samuel and his friends entered Elrond's hut and sat on wooden chairs around a fireplace which had a nice warm fire burning. Elrond made them all a drink of herbal tea. Elrond then went and gathered six spells together.

"What magic do you know Elrond?" Samuel asked.

"I know how to light a dark room and these spell scrolls will be very useful", said Elrond.

After they had all finished their drinks Elrond showed them the way to the Graveyard Keep. They entered the church by the graveyard and Elrond pushed on a statue of a small angel which was decorated on one of the pillars near the alter. A marble slab on the floor slid across to reveal a set of stairs leading down.

"Come on, this way", guided Elrond.

"You first", said Samuel scared it might be a trap set by the king of Draytown to capture them.

"Very well, as you wish it", replied Elrond and descended into the darkness.

The others followed him into a store room full of six barrels of sacramental wine in a small cellar. Two torches on either side of the cellar dimly lit up the room and ahead of them was dark.

"I would never had found the entrance to the crypt if we came without you Elrond", said Samuel.

"Once through there we enter the crypt", said Elrond passing an archway.

Elrond held up his crystal staff and chanted some magic words and the crystal in his staff started to glow. It glowed just enough to see in the darkness. Roger took one of the torches from the cellar wall and followed them from behind as Elrond led the way. Elrond took the right passage. Bats started to fly towards them and attack them. Gillian used his axe to kill the bats with just a few hits. The remaining bats flew away. The passage turned left and more bats attacked them. Samuel and Elrond ducked and some bats flew past them as Gillian tried to hit them but missed. Samuel readied his sword waiting for the bats to swoop down on them again. The bats came back and Samuel, Gillian and John finished them off. They continued up the stone passageway until they came to a wooden door on the left side of the passageway. They entered the door and Samuel's sword crystal started to glow in the handle warning him that undead creatures where nearby. Two zombies were wandering aimlessly around the room. John made the first attack and killed the zombie with ease. The other zombie leered up to attack John and John shielded himself with his arms to avoid the the zombies grasp. Samuel came to his aid and finished the other zombie off.

"Now do you believe me", said Gillian to John.

"Yes, I believe you now. But this is evil magic which has made the dead the living undead", said John.

Elrond started searching around the room.

"Elrond, what are you searching for?" John asked.

"There is a hidden switch in this room which opens a metal gate. We need to find it if we want to continue. Can you help me find it?" Elrond asked.

"Roger noticed one stone sticking up above the others and pushed down on it with his foot. A clanking sound of a chain raising a gate was heard outside of the room.

"That's it Roger, let's go", said Elrond.

"Do, you know this crypt well Elrond?" Samuel asked.

"Only this level. I know how to get down to the next level but I have never been down here before", answered Elrond.

They followed Elrond as he went right into another room. There was a table with a green cloured bottle with a purple coloured liquid inside. John picked it up to examine it.

"Be careful, you don't know what it might be. It could be zombie's blood for all we know", said Elrond.

"Zombie blood, is that bad?" John asked.

"Well if you drunk it thinking it was wine it could turn you into a zombie", replied Elrond.

John placed the bottle carefully back onto the table. Elrond started searching around the room.

"Are you looking for another switch?" Samuel asked.

"No, I'm looking for a red key. It will open the door to another room, which has another switch in it, which opens the last gate. Then we can continue down into the deeper part of the crypt", explained Elrond.

"I have a red key, I found it when we was in the goblin cave", said Samuel.

"Let me see?" Elrond asked. Elrond examined the key. "That's it, that's the one. The goblins must have killed the person that had the key before and then you found it."

"What's the chance of that!" Roger exclaimed.

"Well one in three. There were three keys made", replied Elrond.

Elrond led them back along the passage and took them to the door that was locked. He used the red key and it opened the door. They searched for the switch and pushed it to open the last gate which led down to the lower level of the crypt. They went down the stairs into the lower level of the crypt. Elrond stood at a junction which went left, right and forward.

"Which way now Elrond?" Samuel asked.

"I don't know, I don't know anyone who came down here", answered Elrond. "Maybe we should go right."

They followed Elrond as he took the right path. The floor disappeared under his feet. His staff bridged the gab as he fell into a pit and left Elrond hanging there. John and Gillian helped him up. The rest of them jumped over the pit trap and then continued down the passage which turned left. They came to a door and entered the room. Samuel's sword crystal started to glow again. Three stone tombs were in a long room rested on the floor. The tombs each had a carving of a knight on top of them holding a shield and a sword.

"This is it, we have found the tomb", said John.

Elrond stood there thinking this was too easy to have come to the wizard's tomb so soon. Gillian started to search the first the tomb. Gillian found some red heather which was a red herb.

"What's this?" Gillian asked.

"It's red heather. It is used by wizards for more powerful attack spells. I can make use of that", said Elrond. Gillian gave Elrond the red heather. Elrond placed it in his large bag.

Samuel searched the third tomb and found a root, "What is this?"

"That is also used for a spell. That is used to cause earthquakes and it can also be used to kill zombies", answered Elrond.

John opened the second tomb and a zombie leapt up and grabbed him. John pushed the zombie away.

"Samuel, throw the bane root at the zombie", said Elrond.

Samuel did as Elrond instructed and the bane root hit the zombie making it's skin dry up and turn to ash.

"How come there are zombies down here?" John asked.

"The wizard that cursed this place made the dead alive to protect him while he rested in his tomb. This way it would stop tomb robbers who would be too scared to steal the wizard's treasure", explained Elrond.

They left the room and continued up the passage. They came to another junction and they went left.

"Wait here, I will check for traps up ahead", said Roger. "There is another pit trap, either we turn back or take the other turning."

"It's up to you Samuel, you are in charge", said Elrond.

"Let's take the other turning then", said Samuel and they went back to the other turning following Samuel.

They came to another door and entered a small room. Samuel's sword crystal started to glow. There was a zombie inside and attacked Samuel. Samuel backed against the wall in the small room. The wall turned round and Samuel fell back into a secret room. Gillian threw his axe killing the zombie. John helped Samuel back onto his feet.

"It looks like you have found another secret room", said John.

"This place is full of them", said Samuel brushing off the dust from his clothes.

Samuel saw a wooden stand with plate armour on it. He took the armour off the stand and held it in his arms.

"You take it Samuel, you found it", said John.

Samuel put on the armour, "This will give me some protection."

They rejoined the others in the other room and saw what Samuel had found. Further along the passage they took a turn right at a junction. The passage then turned right. They came to another door and entered the room. Samuel's sword started to glow again to warn of danger. Two zombies wandered around the room and once they saw them started to attack. Gillian killed one with his axe and Roger killed the other with his bow. John could see a chest at the end of the long room and went towards it.

"Wait John, it might be a trap!" Roger shouted.

John heeded Roger's advise and raised his shield to protect himself. A spear shot from the wall near the chest but John was protected by his shield. He opened the chest as the spear from the wall reset itself and John took a bag of gold from the chest and then ran back to the others. John emptied the bag into his hand and counted a 100 gold crowns.

"Well done John", said Samuel.

Roger led them back to an unexplored junction where they had started from before and checked for traps, "All clear!"

A locked red door was at the end of the passageway. Samuel's sword crystal started to glow. Elrond used the red key to unlock the door. A long room with a zombie standing in front of a flowing river stood guard. Elrond killed the zombie with his crystal staff. The small river blocked the path across to the other side of the room where a door was on the other side. Samuel looked into the river and saw piranha fish in the water.

"Piranha fish, we can't cross the river without getting bitten", said Samuel.

"Maybe there is another way to cross the river. Zombie blood is also poisonous. If we use that to kill the fish we can cross", suggested Elrond.

"I remember what room it was in", said John.

"I will go with you, I can warn you off any traps we come across", said Roger.

The others waited by the river while John and Roger returned with the bottle containing zombie blood. Elrond poured the liquid from the bottle into the river. After a few minutes the piranha fish die and float up to the surface. They cross the river safely and enter the door at the far end.

They entered a round room full of statues around the outside. Five candlesticks were spaced around the room. Elornd used magic to light the candles so they could see more clearly. The statues wore robes with a hood over their heads. On the floor was a mosaic of a dragon decorated on the floor in green, red, blue and faint purple. Samuel's sword crystal started to glow brighter than ever warning of more danger.

A voice is head from within the wall, "You must leave now or you shall perish."

"Not until we have what we came for", said Samuel boldly.

"No, no. No one is worthy of my treasure", replied the voice.

Five ghosts came out from the wall and started to move towards them to attack. One ghost past Samuel and swooped into the air and then darted down to attack him.

"These Ghosts are hard to kill", said John.

"Just keep trying", said Samuel.

Gillian threw his axe at one of the ghosts and it went through the ghost and hit one of the statues. Gillian readied his sword. Rogers arrows passed through the ghosts without causing any harm to them. John, Gillian and Samuel killed one each. The remaining two swooped round in the air and attacked Roger wounding him. Elrond chanted some magic words and his hand lit up with fire and shot a fireball at one of the ghosts killing it. He did the same again and finished the other one off. Elrond then fell to his knees weakened.

"Are you okay Elrond?" John asked helping him to his feet.

"Yes, just that the magic took a lot from me, but I'm fine now", replied Elrond.

"Well, we might not have made it this for without you Elrond", said Samuel.

"Thanks", replied Elrond.

"So where's this magic treasure then?" John asked.

Elrond walked over to one of the statues and one was like a knight holding a sword. Elrond pushed down on the sword and a red gem fell out from the sword onto the floor. The dragon picture on the floor had a hole in the eye as if incomplete. Elrond pushed the gem into the eye of the dragon and the knight statue turned round to revel a secret chamber. Inside the chamber was the tomb of the wizard they were looking for. They opened the tomb to find a strange blue glowing steel chain mail.

"This is it. This is the treasure", said Elrond.

"Why does it glow?" John asked.

"It's magic mail that help controls the aura of a wizard giving him protection, and the user is still able to use magic. Most armour can't be worn by wizards as it disrupts a wizards magic aura unless it is magic like this one", explained Elrond.

Samuel picked up the armour and handed it to Elrond, "Take it, you have earned it."

"I don't know what to say", said Elrond.

"Say you will join us and help us on our quest. We need you with your skills of magic and knowledge of herbs, you are a great help to us", said Samuel.

"I will join you. I feel it is my duty, and I feel that I deserve this armour after protecting its secrets after all these years", said Elrond.

"I am one worthy to wear this armour and put it to good use and protect this land from evil", said Elrond.

They left the crypt and travelled back to Elrond's home, a wooden hut near the woods.

"So where do we go from here?" John asked.

"Well with the kings men still after us we will find it hard to continue with our quest. We know the king is in league with the demon lord. If we can attack the castle and kill the king, maybe we can bring peace again", said Samuel.

"But how are we going to do that? The king has guards all over the castle", said John.

"We need to get help from somewhere. We can't do it alone", said Samuel.

"I know where we can find help. We can go to the elves for help, said Elrond.

"Okay then. Tomorrow we travel to the elves", said Samuel.

"I will cook us a meal and then we can all get some rest", said Elrond. "Gillian and Roger, you can fetch some wood for the fire."

"Oh good, some food, I'm hungry", said Gillian.

Chapter 3- The Help of Elves

Samuel and his men travel towards the wood where the elf castle was. They travel north round the outside of some mountains and then travel east past the boarder of another wood on the first day of travel. Elrond tells them stories of a castle keep inside the mountains they past and about a witch that lives in the woodland that they pass.

"You have many stories about these parts Elrond", said John.

"Oh, I only know this area a little bit. The father east I know nothing about", said Elrond.

After a days travelling it starts to get dark. Roger hunts for wild boar and kills one with his bow.

Gillian and John collect wood for a fire. Roger makes a fire and they cook the wild boar Roger caught on the fire.

"So what do you know about these elves?" John asked Elrond.

"Well, I know my master was friends with them. They taught him a bit about magic I think. I went with him a few times to collect rare herbs from them. They know me, so we should be all right", answered Elrond.

They laid under their sheep skin rugs and slept in a circle around the dying ambers of the fire.

The next morning they awoke and picked some wild berries and some apples from a nearby tree. They ate these for breakfast and continued on their journey led by Elrond. They passed a stone circle made up of tall stones. In the circle were smaller stones.

"What's that?" John asked.

"It's a stone circle. Witches and wizards met here at night at special times of the year to practice magic. There is a legend that one wizard using a magic stone could make himself appear inside the circle", answered Elrond.

"Strange!" John exclaimed.

Soon they came to the edge of Elf Wood. As they drew deeper into the woodland it became thick with trees. A small path appeared from a small clearing in the woodland. Eight elves armed with bows surround them. They had all their bows aimed at them.

"I thought you were friends with the elves?" John asked.

"Why do you trespass into elvish woodland humans?" One of the elves in front of them asked aiming his bow right at Samuel.

"We came to the king to ask for help and we have a message for him", spoke Elrond.

"Elrond" The wizard's apprentice?" The elf questioned.

"Yes, I am", replied Elrond.

"Forgive me, we are suspicious of strangers, I didn't recognize you at first with all these others with you", said the elf. "We will take you to the king. Follow us."

They followed the elves along the path.

"So who are these travellers that you bring with you Elrond?" The elf asked.

"These are my new found friends. They are on a quest to destroy evil from this land. And I have joined them in their quest", replied Elrond.

"Well there is a lot of evil to the east, and it is no easy task for a man or an elf to free this land of evil. You must have some very brave men. My name is Torell", introduced the elf.

They came to a clearing in the woods. The wood continued around the whole landscape like a protection of trees. They crossed a small bridge that went over a small flowing river. The elf castle stood in the distance on top of a green hill. A wall guarded with tall turrets surrounded the castle. Another wall raised above that one was further inwards, and the elf palace was inside another wall inside that one. The castle shone white with its clear clean stone. They entered under a large gate with two wooden carved doors. They were brought before the elvish king.

"What news do you bring me and what help do you ask of me?" The elf king asked.

"The Royal Castle near our village of Draytown has an evil king. He is working for the demon lord in the east in the black mountains in the Barren Wastes. I have been given a map to help defeat him and I know of a sword that can defeat this demon lord. This is our quest, but we need your help in attacking the castle and killing this evil king. He has been hunting us because he knows we have this map. We can not continue on our quest if we are being hunted by this evil king. If you help us defeat this king we can continue with our quest without any hindrance from Royal Castle", said Samuel.

"What prove do you have that this king in the Royal Castle of men is evil?" The elf king asked.

"We was captured and John saw the king talking to the demon lord with the help of a crystal ball", said Samuel.

"It's true, I saw it with my own eyes and he wanted to kill us all because of the map", said John.

"I can not help you with just the prove of your words. I can not war against humans unless it is for good reason, especially Royal Castle. However, I have a way of proving your words. Guards, bring the crystal ball of truth", ordered the elf king.

The guards brought in a small chest and unlocked it and pulled out a white crystal ball that shimmered green, blue and purple.

"Gather round and we will see. Crystal ball of truth and light show us the true nature of the king of Royal Castle", requested the elf king.

The crystal ball showed the king of Royal Castle and then showed a dark shadowy demon inside the king like a dark evil spirit.

"The ball of truth has shown us that your words a true. We must act to help you. You will have sixty of my men to attack the castle, but it will be up to you to kill the king. If word got out that elves had killed the king we would be in danger of attack from your kind", said the elf king.

"Very well", replied Samuel.

"You will stay with us inside our palace under our protection until our men are readied for battle", said the elf king.

"Thank you", said Samuel.

"Torell, you will go with them and oversee the armies", ordered the elf king.

"Very well, sire", replied Torell.

Torell showed them to their rooms. They ate with the king fish and fresh fruit and had apple pie for desert. Samuel and his men, rested well that night in Elf Castle in wooden beds.

The next morning Torrel woke Samuel and his men, "The king wishes to see you Samuel."

Samuel followed Torell along the twisting corridors of the castle which led to the kings chamber,

"Torell can I ask you something?" Samuel asked.

"Yes, ask away", replied Torell.

"How did your people become elves, I mean what made you an elf?" Samuel asked.

"Well, the first elf was made from a fairy. Once long ago a fairy fell in love with a human. This human was beautiful and had a most distinguished face. She used her fairy magic to appear human and the human fell in love with the fairy and with her charm and beauty. Their union together made the first elf. And that's the story", explained Torell.

"That's so beautiful. So are all elves good in nature?" Samuel asked.

"Not all. Our people stay away from humans. We embrace nature and use our skills to beautify our castle and homes. We help the weak if we are travelling outside the village, and if we happen to come across humans we try not to interfere with them unless we see them in need of help. But there are the dark elves that have given themselves to evil. They despise elves and humans alike. They hunger for war and attack the weak and steal and work dark magic like the chaos wizards. They keep to themselves just like us. We keep away from them but if they see an elf or human they kill them out of hatred", answered Torell.

"So why are they like that?" Samuel asked.

"There once was a prince to the king. An elfish prince, and he wanted the kingdom for himself. He killed the king and wanted the crystal of truth to find his enemies within the castle and have them killed so no one could stand in his way. When one day, one of the guards that guarded the crystal of truth saw it glow and opened the chest to look at the crystal ball. It showed him the true intent of the prince and how he killed the king. The guard ran and told the others within the castle. When they confronted the price he was angry and ordered his men to kill these men, because they wanted to take the royal throne for themselves and they made up lies against him. There was a battle within the castle and the guard showed them what the crystal of truth showed him. They got an army together and forced the prince with his followers out of the land. That's how the dark elves became. They teach their children to hate other elves and humans because they were robbed of the throne, and the kingdom, and of the crystal of truth", answered Torell.

They entered the kings chamber.

"Step forward Samuel", requested the elf king.

Samuel walked forward and knelt on a red carpet below some steps before the elf king.

"Take these elvish cloaks, it will give you some protection on your quest. They are made from burrow worm thread. It is all I have to offer you on your quest", said the king.

"Thank you", said Samuel receiving the elvish cloaks.

Samuel returned to the others and gave the cloaks to his men. At the end of the week the elves were prepared to attack Royal Castle. They journeyed together with the elves to attack Royal Castle.

"What is your plan Samuel?" Torell asked.

"I just need your men to attack the castle wall and keep the soldiers busy. They will then move their guards from other areas from the castle to help protect the main gate. Myself and my men will then sneak into the river system that leads into the castle and fight our way to the kings chamber. Once we are inside the kings chamber we will kill the king. Once the king is dead we will blow on a horn to call off the attack", answered Samuel.

"Well, may the strength of the elves be with you on your task", said Torell.

Torell ordered his archers to take aim at the castle guards along the wall. They managed to kill six soldiers on the wall on the first strike. The soldiers on the castle wall hid behind their shields to shield them from the next attack of arrows.

"Aim high", ordered Torell to his men.

The arrows flew high into the air and dropped down on the soldiers on the wall and on the ground behind the wall. Four more soldiers were killed when the arrows hit them in the chest and head. The other soldiers were protected by their helmets as the arrows came from above.

Samuel took his men to the back of the castle and walked behind some bushes to hide from the view of the soldiers on the wall of the castle.

"Now how do we get across the river without being seen?" Gillian asked.

"A man goes fishing in the moat. We can use his boat", said John.

"John are you sure a man uses his boat to go fishing here?" Samuel asked John.

"Yes he's usually here at this time in the morning", replied John.

As they went through the bushes they could see the boat. They climbed into the boat and waded across the moat towards the castle.

A soldier spotted them and fired some arrows at their boat. He fired three shots one after another and they all missed but the arrows came close to the side of their boat. Roger took careful aim and fired an arrow killing him. They entered the water system which ran through a small tunnel under the castle. They entered the castle the same way as they had escaped from the castle with John's help. Elrond used a light spell to see through the darkness of the tunnel. They came to a stone path running by the sewers and all got out from the boat. John tired the boat to a metal post. Gillian climbed up and attached a rope so the others could climb up into the castle. They came to the prison of the castle and Gillian and John fought and killed two guards. Another two guards came running towards them. Samuel swung his sword and killed one of them and Gillian swung overhead killing the other one.

"Please let me go free, I have been wronged by the king", said a man dressed in brown and black clothes calling out from behind one of the prison cells.

"Why have you been imprisoned here?" Samuel asked.

"I was caught stealing a crystal ball from the kings secret chamber", said the man.

"I'm not letting any thief go free, it's not the sort of thing I would do?" Samuel replied.

"Please wait, I know the secret of the king, please hear me first, I beg of you sire", pleaded the man.

"Come on Samuel, we have no time to listen to stories from a common thief", suggested John.

"So why are you here? You didn't come through the gate and you killed the kings guards. You are no better than me", shouted the thief.

"Okay, tell us what happened", agreed Samuel wishing to keep the man silent and not wanting to alert any more attention to themselves.

"I broke into the kings secret chamber and took a quick look around to see if there was anything worth stealing that might be of some value, when I saw a crystal ball on the table. I picked it up and carried it under my arm. The crystal started to glow and I panicked and it fell onto the floor, and I saw a demon face appear in the crystal ball. I think the king is in league with a demon. When the ball hit the ground the kings guards heard and entered the chamber and threw me into prison. Oh, what's the point of telling you all this, you don't believe me", said the man.

"We believe you", said Samuel. "Roger, get the key and let this man go free", said Samuel.

"Why do you believe me", said the man surprised.

"We are on a quest to kill the king. We know he is in league with the demon lord. He imprisoned us too. The king is working for this demon lord and has sought after us and he wants to kill us if he captures us. We are on a quest to find a magical sword that can kill this demon lord but the king is halting our progress by hunting after us. Once we kill the king he will not be able to stand in our way any more and we can continue with our quest", explained Samuel.

"My name is Jumbo Jack, I am very grateful to you, for freeing me. I hope you all do well in your quest. All I can offer you in thanks is this; I am fleeing to the city of Theb and if I hear anything about this sword I will let you know. Just visit me there", said Jumbo.

"Why do they call you Jumbo Jack?" Samuel asked.

"My real name is Jack, they just call me Jumbo because I'm small. It's just some kind of jokey nickname", replied Jumbo.

Jumbo went through the door of the prison and went his way while Samuel took his men into the corridor towards the kings hall. Soldiers in light armour and triangle shaped shields attacked them. They fought four soldiers. They came to the door of the kings hall. Two guards armed with pike staffs guarded the door. Elrond cast a fire spell which hit the door smashing it into flames and ashes. The two guards fled in fear. They entered the kings hall. The king stood up from his throne.

"How dare you enter my kingdom!" The king exclaimed.

He drew his sword ready for battle.

"We know you are working for the demon lord, we saw the crystal ball. Now you must die you traitor to the royal kingdom", said Samuel boldly drawing his sword.

"Then you must all die and after your deaths the demon lord will have the map safely in his grasp again", said the king.

Samuel fought with the king and he was quite skilled with the sword. After thirty minutes of fighting the king felt tired and rested on his sword to catch his breath. Samuel thrust his sword at the king. The king defended Samuel's attack but was too weak to defend his next attack and Samuel stabbed the king in the chest. The king fell to the floor.

The princess and daughter of the king came with twelve guards into the kings hall to defend the king. When she saw her father fallen to the floor she ran to his side.

"What have you done?" The princess said in disgust.

At that moment a dark shadowy ghostly figure emerged from the king and flew into the air screaming with a hollow cry and disappeared through one of the windows above.

"Forgive me my daughter, a demon fought with me and took over my body. I was too old to fight him off and became under his spell and worked for the demon lord. Please forgive me?" The king pleaded.

"Oh father", said the princess.

"The kingdom is once free from evil, please promise me to keep it this way", said the king.

"I promise father", said the princess.

The king died and the princess wept.

"You was right, I know you didn't have much of a choice. Who ever you are?", asked the princess looking at Samuel with tears in her eyes.

"I am Samuel", was his only reply.

The princesses personal servant and priestess entered the room, "What is happening, the castle is under attack."

Roger went up the to the wall of the castle and blew on the horn that he took from one of the goblins when they attack the goblin leader at the Goblin Caves to signal the death of the king which was the signal for the elves to call off the attack.

Then Roger returned to the hall.

"You and your men must leave now", said the princess. "I must rebuild my fathers kingdom again and bring him honour."

"I understand", said Samuel and took his men and rejoined with the elves.

"What happened my lady?" Her servant asked.

"My father was taken over by an evil spirit which made him serve the dark lord. I saw the demon left my fathers body and my father asked me to keep the kingdom free from evil. For some reason this Samuel knew that my father had been taken over by a demon and fought and killed my father to try and return peace to the kingdom", explained the princess.

"This man must have the gift of prophecy to know such things", said the servant.

"Maybe", said the princess.

"I would like to know more about this man", said her servant.

At the demon lord's castle the dark shadow ghost that possessed the king returned to tell the news of what had happened.

"My lord the king of Royal Castle near Draytown is dead. I can no longer control the area. The kings daughter will soon be crowned queen and rule over the kingdom", said the shadow ghost.

"I will send my armies of orcs to destroy Draytown and after that my armies of orcs will sweep across the land until I have that map in my grasp again", said the demon lord.

Back at Samuel's town the Potters Den, Samuel said, "Thank you for your help Torell and the help of the elves."

"My elves are returning to the Elf Castle. I want to become part of your group and help you on your quest", requested Torell.

"Yes you can join us on our quest, we need the help", said Samuel.

They all went to the tavern to celebrate. The princess was crowned queen in her kingdom and all celebrated across town.

Towards the evening of the celebration of the princess becoming queen an elf rode into Potters Den.

"Towns people, I bring news of an army of orcs. They are heading this way towards Draytown. Our elves are going to try to cut them off at the mountain pass. Now I must go and warn Royal Castle", said the elf and fled.

"What are we going to do?" One of the villagers said.

"This is all your doing Samuel", complained one of the villagers.

Gillian stood up to speak, "You say that Samuel has brought this upon the village but I say he has brought freedom. Samuel defeated the demon spirit that took over the king which brought an evil rule to this land. Now his daughter will rule this land as queen and protect us from this evil where before the king was being controlled by the demon lord."

"So what should we do then Samuel?" One of the villagers asked.

"We will fight to protect Potters Den. And any others that can fight to protect us should join us", said Samuel.

The towns people returned their homes to lock their homes and boarded up their windows. Some of the towns people got weapons and joined Samuel and his men.

A women rode on horse back followed by twelve royal soldiers on horse back and another twenty on foot following behind.

"I am servant of the queen, my name is Sarah. I have been sent by the queen with a few of her soldiers to help defend Potters Den. The queen also is preparing to protect the castle", said Sarah.

Samuel helped Sarah down from her horse. "We are grateful for your help."

"I wanted to protect you and your men, and I asked the queen if I could come myself and she granted my wish", said Sarah.

Samuel and Sarah prepared their troops to surround the outside of Potters Den ready for the orcs attack.

Another elf on horseback rode into Potters Den, "The orcs have been attacked at the mountain pass. Many have been killed but a few got through and are heading this way. Another army of orcs have been reported coming from the south and are heading this way", said the elf.

The elf rode off towards Royal Castle to warn them of the orc army as well.

Five hours later the army of orcs arrived and attacked Potters Den. The orcs had swords and wore chain mail with leather jackets over the top. A few were armed with shields. Sarah and her soldiers worked together to fight off the orcs. A few orcs entered the town and fired fire arrows which they had lit to set fire to the houses. The villagers tried to put out the fires while other villagers attacked the orcs who had managed to enter the town. The orcs were defeated and had lost most of their soldiers and had started to flee. A few royal soldiers had been wounded and some had been wounded from Potters Den. Even Roger had been wounded in the arm by an orc blade. Sarah had fought with a spear and strapped it to the side of her horse saddle after the battle was over. She went over to the ones most wounded and placed her hands together forming a shape of a triangle with her hands. Light energy glowed around her hands and helped heal and sealed their bleeding wounds. She took a look at Roger and tied a bandage around his arm.

"Here you go, your wound is not too bad, you should recover in a day or two", said Sarah.

"You can heal by magic", Samuel said amazed.

"Yes, I'm a priestess. I was taught at the church in the castle. I can only use my power a few times as it draws a lot of energy. I hope it has helped save the lives of the most wounded", said Sarah.

"That was some great magic", said Elrond.

"Each teacher can teach magic differently, I have been taught in the healing arts", said Sarah.

"Yes, but you was good in combat as well", said Elrond.

"So was you, I saw you destroy a couple of orcs with your fireball magic", said Sarah.

"Sarah we could use your help, will you join us?" Samuel asked.

"I would love to help you on your quest", said Sarah.

"Your healing skills could help a lot especially if we get wounded in battle", said Samuel.

"I was hoping I could join you, I have already told the queen I wanted to join you", said Sarah.

"Oh that's good. I will tell the others", said Samuel.

"Men, Torell the elf and Sarah the priestess is going to join us on our quest."

Samuel's men welcomed Sarah and Torell into their group. The villagers thanked Sarah and Samuel for saving their town from the orcs. Potter's Den lost three houses due to the attack and the villagers started to repair the damage to their village. At the end of the week they celebrated the safety of their village.

The next day Samuel got his team together ready with food supplies which they carried on Sarah's horse and headed north. They travelled north towards the stone circle.

They came to a village called North Stow. It had a wooden fence around the village. The houses were made out of dark wooden timbers. The whole village looked dark and dreary.

The villagers looked sad and weary. When they saw Samuel and his friends they turned away and made them feel unwelcome. Samuel thought that the villagers did not like strangers coming to their village.

"Not much of a village is this", said John.

"We just need to find somewhere to stay and rest for the night", said Samuel not wanting to stay for long.

Roger stopped a man carrying water from a well, "Excuse me, do you know if there is any where we can stay and rest in this village?"

The man just pointed to a tavern with a broken sign hanging on a chain.

"Thank you", replied Roger.

"I could do with a drink", said Gillian.

They entered the tavern and bought a drink for themselves.

"It seems very strange this village", said Sarah.

"I know what you mean", said Roger.

"Why do you think that is?" Samuel asked Sarah.

"Well didn't you think it was strange, I haven't seen any children outside", said Elrond.

"I have noticed that as well", said Torell.

Sarah went up to the bar to get the next round of drinks, "Barmen, where are all the children in this village?"

The other villagers heard this and gave Sarah the evil eye look and then turned their backs on her.

"They should be all locked up", said the barmen firmly.

"But why?" Sarah asked.

"You best not ask too many questions around here. The village is in a sad state and the less you ask about it the better the people will feel if you just keep your nose out of their affairs", replied the barmen.

Sarah retuned to the table with their drinks.

"What was that all about?" Gillian asked.

"Best not ask", said Sarah.

At that moment a woman came into the bar crying, "Somebody help me."

The barmen went over to the woman and said, "Calm down, we will sort it all out in the morning. We have visitors you don't want to scare them away now. Now go home and I will talk to you in the morning."

"But what are we going to do?" The woman asked still upset.

"Don't worry, I will talk to you in the morning", said the barman.

The woman left the tavern still upset and still crying.

"What was going on there?" Roger asked.

"I don't know", said Samuel.

"Well you head what the barmen said we should just ignore it", said Sarah.

"Anyway, tomorrow we will be on our way", said Samuel.

Samuel spoke to the barman, "Do you have any rooms me and my friends can stay in for the night?"

"As long as it is not more than four days and it will cost you 60 gold crowns for all of you", replied the barman.

"Yes, that is fine", said Samuel paying the barman the price he set.

The next morning they got up and got dressed had a drink and something to eat from the tavern. They went outside to get some fresh air.

"Hey Samuel isn't that the woman who we saw in the tavern last night crying", said Roger.

"Yes it is", replied Samuel.

"I wonder what the barmen is saying to her?" Roger asked.

"We better get our supplies so we can get going", said Samuel.

The barmen passed them and entered the tavern. The woman came up to them.

"Please Sirs, can you help me. My daughter has gone missing and the village people are too afraid to help any more", said the woman.

"Why, what has happened?" Roger asked.

"In the woods which is north of the village there lives an evil witch. She steals children from the village and I have heard she sacrifices them to her idol god. The villages have gone to her lair to kill her but none have ever returned. Now the villagers live in fear and lock their children inside their homes to try and protect them. Please can you help me and I will reward you with one hundred gold crowns", the woman explained.

"Yes we will help you", said Samuel.

"We better tell the others", said Roger.

Roger went inside the tavern and took them outside and told them of the woman's pleas. They headed north into the woods near the village and entered an old castle. Torches lit the walls. Water dripped down the walls and green slime covered parts of the floor.

"This place gives me chills", said John.

Two goblins guarded a large wooden door. Roger took aim with his bow and killed the goblin by hitting it in the chest. Sarah ran towards the other and attacked with her spear and killed it. They opened the door and walked inside. The passageway was dark and four blobs of slime attacked them. Gillian, John, Samuel and Sarah attacked them. They killed the blobs and took a look around the courtyard. There was a tower in the distance with a light on.

"That tower up there could be where the witch is", said Samuel.

"We need to go up those stairs to reach it", said John.

Two goblin archers fired arrows from the wall above. Samuel and his team took cover. Torell and Roger took aim with their bows. They took cover behind a broken pillar which once supported the roof. They killed the goblins and continued up the stairs. They came to a stone arched bridge which had many cracks in it. Goblins came running at them from behind. They ran across the bridge. Four goblins waited on the other side. Gillian, Samuel, Sarah and John fought them. They came to another bridge. This time it was an old rope bridge with wooden boards for the flooring of the bridge.

"More goblins are coming", warned Sarah.

Elrond fired a fire ball at one of them killing them.

"We must go across the bridge, there is no other way", said Samuel.

"It doesn't look safe", said Roger.

"What other choice do we have", said Samuel.

They went across the bridge and one of the goblins cut the bridge. The bridge started to fall and they all fell through a wooden floor below that was rotten from the weather and collapsed beneath them. They all fell again into the lower dungeon.

John fell on his back with the weight of his armour, "I think I have hurt my back in the fall."

"Let me help", said Sarah and used a heal spell on his back.

"Thank you, all the pain has gone", said John.

"Your welcome", said Sarah.

Everyone got to their feet. They could see where they had broken through the old rotten floor from above where they had fell. Light streamed through the broken floor from above given some light around them.

"It looks like a passage leads ahead", said Roger.

"We have to find a way to get back to that tower", said Samuel.

They came to a turning that went left and right. Roger checked for traps and gave the all clear. They took the left passage which felt damp and cold. Samuel's sword started to glow. Samuel drew his sword ready to face whatever undead monster would appear. A ghost came out from the wall behind them and attacked them from behind. John, Samuel and Roger was all startled at first because they where leading from the front. The ghost groaned and turned to attack Gillian. Gillian used an overhead swing to kill the ghost.

"That seemed easy to kill", said Gillian.

"These ghosts must have been summoned here by the witches dark magic to protect these halls", suggested Elrond.

The passage turned right and led to a door. Samuel opened the door carefully. Inside was a small square room with a chest hovering high in the air.

"What kind of magic is this?" John asked.

"It's a levitation spell. It's used to stop thieves stealing from wizards. It's quite a simple spell, I should be able to cancel the spell", said Elrond.

Elrond used a levitation spell to bring the chest down to the ground. Inside the chest was a silver necklace with a skull on it with two glowing green gem eyes fixed into it.

"What is it?" Samuel asked.

"It's a protection of the undead. Any one who wears it has no fear of them and can't be harmed by decaying flesh from zombies or mummies", answered Elrond.

"I think you should have it Samuel as Gillian already has the amulet of courage", said Elrond and hanged the chain around his neck.

They left the room and continued up the passage. Samuel's sword crystal started to glow again. Another ghost appeared from the wall. Torell fired an arrow at the ghost and it went right through it. Gillian attacked the ghost killing it. They continue until they come to another door which was on the right and enter it. They entered a small square room, damp with water dripping down the sides of the room. In the middle of the room was a frog. It jumped onto Elrond's shoulder.

"Let's kill it", said Gillian.

"It seems harmless, and it's only one frog", said Elrond.

Gillian tried to grab the frog, but it jumped off onto Torell's shoulder. Gillian tried to catch the frog and it jumped onto the floor and hid in a dark crack in the wall.

"Just leave it Gillian", said Samuel.

Gillian was just angry such a small thing could beat him.

They left the room and left the frog behind them. But as soon as they walked round to the next passage way the frog followed them.

"You again hey", said Gillian.

"Maybe it's trying to tell us something", said Torell.

"I will use an understanding spell", said Elrond.

All of a sudden the frog could speak, "Please help me. I was turned into a frog by that evil witch. My friends also have been turned into frogs. I came here to save my daughter who was kidnapped and brought a group of four others with me. An evil witch caught us and turned us all into frogs. I managed to escape and have been hiding down here ever since but no one could understand me until now. Please help me!"

"Well, would you look at that!" Gillian exclaimed.

"I will led you to a grate that leads back up to the next level. Follow me", said the frog.

They followed the frog to a room and on the floor was a grate with iron bars.

John tried to pull it open but it was too tight. Gillian tried but it was to tight.

"I think it's locked", said Gillian.

Elrond used a light spell to see into the grate, "I can see a grey key below."

"Can you reach it?" Samuel asked.

"No, its too far down", said Elrond. "Someone must have locked it and then thrown away the key down there."

"I can get it", said the frog and hopped through the grate, grabbed the key in it's mouth and hoped back through the grate.

Elrond took the key and opened the grate. They climbed down into the dark passage. Elrond cast a light spell so they could see. At the end of the passage was a set of stone stairs leading up.

"I will find a way out and wait for you outside until you kill that nasty old witch", said the frog.

They climb up the stairs and come to a dead end with a door to the right. They enter the room and find a cupboard. On the floor was a pile of bones. As Elrond moves towards the cupboard the pile of bones spring to life to form a skeleton holding a sword. The skeleton pushes Elrond to the side.

Samuel with his undead amulet protection felt brave enough to attack the skeleton and killed it. John helped Elrond get back onto his feet. Elrond discovers a health potion and takes it from the cupboard. Samuel's sword started to glow to warn of more danger ahead. They enter through another door to the next room and find a skeleton guarding a weapons rack. John, Gillian and Samuel fought with the skeleton and killed it. Elrond finds a staff with a glowing orb at the top of it from the weapons rack.

"What have you found Elrond?" John asks.

"It is an orb staff. Better than my crystal staff. It has magical powers within it to help regain lost magic", replied Elrond. Elrond held up the staff and a glowing yellow light shone from it and Elrond felt some of his magic restored. "I feel my lost magic has returned."

"There's no way forward we have to turn back", said Roger searching the wall for any hidden doors.

They return to the passageway stairs where they came from and Roger searched the walls again and finds a secret door. Samuel's sword crystal starts to glow again. They enter a small room which leads to another door with another skeleton inside. They kill it and come to another door which is locked when John tries to open it. Samuel tries the red key and it opens. They enter a large room with a table in the centre. It is dusty and looks like it hasn't been used for years. John takes a small bag which was on the table and empties it. Dust falls out.

"I can use this to carry more coinage", said John.

Roger searches for a secret wall and it leads out onto a bridge. There is a gap in the middle which is too far to jump across.

"That frog has led us into a dead end", said Gillian.

"Elrond can you use a levitation spell to get us all across?" Samuel asks.

"Only for a couple of people", answered Elrond.

"I'm going to try to jump it", said Gillian. Gillian took a long run up and took a long jump, and fell short and thought he was going to fall. Gillian fell against the bridge on his face.

"It was an illusion", said Elrond.

John walked along the bridge where Gillian fell, "Nice try."

Gillian got back to his feet and said "I'm going to kill that witch when I find her."

Once across the bridge of illusion they reached a door. Samuel's sword started to glow again.

They opened the door and there were two skeletons ready to attack them. The skeletons raised their swords in the air and attacked. Torell fired an arrow at the skeleton and it hit him in the eye socket of his skull. As the skeleton tried to pull it out Gillian slashed his sword slicing the skeleton in half and it fell to the floor in pieces. Roger fired an arrow at the other skeleton. The arrow stuck in the skeletons rib cage. The skeleton snapped the stuck arrow in half. John attacked the skeleton and finished it off. After the skeletons were killed they searched for a secret door that would lead out.

"Maybe that frog was the witch and led us the wrong way", said Gillian.

"There must be a secret door somewhere, keep looking", said Samuel.

"I've found it", said Elrond and pushed the wall open.

The secret door led to a passageway that turned to the right. A red dressed wizard stood by the stairs that led up to the witches tower.

"None shall pass and live", said the red wizard and fired fireball towards them. The first attack from the wizard missed. The wizard fired again and the fireball flew towards

Samuel. Samuel defended with his wooden shield. The fireball exploded and flames just fell from the surface of Samuels shield. Torell fired an arrow at the red wizard. It hit him in the chest and he fell dead.

They climbed the steps to the witches tower. Elrond ran forward and fell down a trap. His orb staff bridge the pit and he just lay there hanging. Torell helped Elrond climb out.

"Thank you Torell", thanked Elrond.

They jumped across the pit trap. The passage turned to the right and was met by another red wizard. The red wizard threw a fireball at Roger. Roger dodged the fireball which impacted against the wall. Torell took aim and killed the red wizard. Roger checked along the passageway for more traps. He discovered another pit trap. They all jumped across the pit trap and followed the passage until it went round to the right. Another red wizard was standing waiting for them. It fired a fireball towards Samuel. Samuel defended with his shield. Sarah threw her spear and it struck the wizard in the chest. She ran to the dead wizard and pulled out her spear from his chest. They entered a door on the right which led into a large room. Samuel's sword started glow to warn of danger. Two red wizards and a skeleton was in the room. Sarah attacked one of the wizards with her spear. The other wizard fired a fireball which hit John's armour but he was unhurt. Torell fired an arrow at the red wizard while Gillian attacked the skeleton. After they had killed the wizards and the skeleton, Elrond found on the table a magic potion.

"What is it?" John asked.

"It looks like an anti-magic potion", said Elrond. Elrond took the potion and they entered the passageway again as there were no more exits. Roger found a secret door. Samuel's sword crystal started to glow again.

"Careful Roger, my sword senses danger in the room.

He entered it and a ghost attacked him. Elrond entered the room and fired a fireball at the ghost killing it. They left the small room through a door that led into another small room with no exits.

"Let's search for another secret door I suppose", said Gillian.

As Gillian stepped onto the floor a dart fired from the wall and hit his arm. Gillian backed up into the other room and Sarah took a look at Gillian's wound. Sarah used her magic to heal Gillian, "There you go, all better again."

"Thank you", thanked Gillian.

Roger crept around the edge of the wall searching for a hidden door. He found one that led into another room. Samuel's sword crystal started to glow. Two ghost flew out from the wall. Sarah attacked one ghost with her spear and Elrond fired another fireball killing the other. Samuel's sword was still glowing.

"There must still be more undead monsters ahead", warned Samuel.

"Let me guess, more ghosts", said Gillian.

They entered the next room which was a large hall. The witch stood at the far end. Two metal cages were hanging from the ceiling. One had skeleton bones inside and the other had a girl inside. Two ghosts stood next to the witch wearing a metal helmet and chest plate armour and were armed with a staff axe. On a table was a large bowl of frogs.

"How dare you enter my lair. I don't know how you got here but now prepare to die", screamed the witch. "Guards attack them!"

The two ghost guards drifted above the floor and attacked John and Samuel. Sarah and Gillian helped fight the ghost guards.

"Your next witch", said Gillian.

After the ghosts where killed Gillian walked forward across a magic floor circle. A mystic orb fired a bolt of lighting hitting Gillian as he entered the circle.

"I don't think so", said the witch laughing.

Elrond drunk the magic potion which he found earlier and crossed the circle unharmed.

"I don't believe it. Okay so you're a wizard but you won't catch me", said the witch.

Elrond took a swing at the witch with his orb staff and she disappeared. The witch reappeared on the other side of the room. Torell took aim and fired. The witch disappeared again. Elrond held his orb staff above his head and it charge with lighting and then fired the lighting bolt at the witch when she reappeared. The lighting hit the witch killing her. The frogs on the table turned back into humans who where from the village of North Stow.

"Thank you for saving us from the curse of the witch", said one of the villagers.

One of the villagers went over to the body of the dead witch and took a grey key from her neck and opened the cage with the girl inside, "Your safe now Becky."

Elrond searched behind the witches throne that she sat on and found a helmet.

"I recognize that helmet. That was stolen from our village", said Torell. "It's a magic helmet called the fear helmet. It has protection against ghosts and skeletons. It is said only wizards and elves can wear it. You should keep it as a thank you for saving our lives."

"Then you should have it", said Elrond and passed the helmet to Torell.

They left the witches lair and found another villager outside who had also been turned into a frog.

"Thanks for saving me and the other villagers" said the villager.

They headed back to North Stow. Becky's mother greeted them at the gate and thanked them all for their bravery. The villagers wives also thanked them for returning their lost husbands. The village gave them one hundred gold as a reward. With the money they bought John a knight shield, and Roger some chain mail. They celebrated in the tavern with a free drink from the village and free food for that night. They also could sleep in the tavern for free that night.

That night Samuel took out the map and the diary he had found in the man's home, the same man who had given him the map. He had the first key to unlock one of the gates in the Seventh Tower.

"So this is the map then", said Sarah.

"Yes and we have already got the first key", said Samuel.

"So Samuel do you think the witch has something to do with the keys because she had a locked red door only the red key could open?" John asked.

"Maybe she once had the red key and it belonged to her before the goblins took it. Or maybe the goblins were friends of the witch and they both used the key. We did come across goblin archers in the witches lair. And she did have help from some red wizards defending her lair. Or maybe they both had a red key and was guarding it for the demon lord.", suggested Samuel.

"So where does the diary say the next key is hidden?"

"The diary says that it is hidden in a pyramid deep in the desert. It says it is guarded by an undead mummy warrior who lived there six hundred years ago. And an evil wizard brought him back to life when he was searching for the key for himself. The undead warrior tried to kill the evil wizard for disturbing his eternal rest and the evil wizard trapped the undead warrior inside the pyramid", explained Samuel.

"So we need to find a way into the pyramid then", said Torell.

"Well tomorrow we can start the journey east to the desert", said Samuel.

Chapter 4- The Pyramid

The next morning Samuel and his team bought some food supplies and collected some water from the village well for the journey east towards the desert. They pass below the stone circle and after a couple of hours travelling they reach the edge of the desert. They set up their tents and build a fire from dry bracken around the camp area. The next morning they head into the desert. They pass a traders tent who has a stall of pots and sells them some water supplies and some dates and fresh fruit. Samuel notices a man dressed in a shabby shawl steal an apple and run off with it. Samuel chases after the thief. Samuel's friends follow Samuel as he chases after the thief. After going over four dunes Samuel catches the thief and grabs hold of him.

"Let me go!" The thief shouted.

"Why was you stealing?" Samuel asked.

"I was hungrey", replied the thief.

"That's no excuse. I should take you back to that stall and tell the man what you have done", said Samuel.

"Please sir let me go, if they punish me for stealing they will cut off my hand. Please have mercy on me kind sir it was only an apple", pleaded the thief.

"I guess I should, you have done little harm and I would hate for you to lose your hand on my account", said Samuel.

"Thank you kind sir. I tell you what, I have a map for sale. It shows of a secret entrance into the great pyramid", said the thief.

"Can we trust him Samuel, he is a thief", said John.

"Let me see?" Samuel asked.

The thief took from his belt a scroll and showed it to Samuel. Samuel examined the scroll and could see a map showing the hidden entrance.

"See it is a secret entrance. I myself have used it to get inside the pyramid. I found a gold helmet inside that I sold to a shop in the city of Theb for a good price. They say there are many treasures inside but there are a few traps that were too dangerous for me so I don't venture there any more", said the thief.

"Okay, how much for the map?" Samuel asked.

"50 gold crowns", replied the thief.

"I will give you 20", said Samuel.

"All right, I don't need it any more anyway", said the thief.

Samuel gave the thief the money and he gave Samuel the map.

"Don't forget, you will need a spade to dig into that pyramid because the secret entrance will be covered by sand by now", said the thief.

The thief walked into the distance and Samuel and his team went back to the stall and bought a spade for 10 gold crowns. They went back into the desert and found the great pyramid.

"Well have you ever seen such a monument so large!" Gasped John.

"No, never", said Samuel.

Roger searched around the outside of the pyramid. It's walls were so smooth except for a fake stone door at the front.

"There's no way in", said Roger.

"Well let's see if this map shows where the secret entrance is", said Samuel. "Gillian, dig over there by the south of the pyramid.

"But it's just sand", said Gillian.

"Trust me, that's what the map says", said Samuel.

"At least it is in the shade", said Gillian.

Gillian started digging and came to hard stone after digging for three hours.

"Gillian's found the entrance!" Roger shouted.

There were some broken stones around where the hidden entrance was. Elrond went down some stone steps and used a light spell to see into the passageway.

"Well, what do you see Elrond?" Samuel asked.

"This is it, the entrance leads down into the great pyramid", replied Elrond.

They all went down into the passageway and saw ancient hieroglyphs written on the walls.

"Elrond, can you read this ancient text written on these walls?" Torell asked.

"I can with an understanding spell", said Elrond.

Elrond cast an understanding spell and a green light shined against the wall making Elrond able to read the hieroglyhs.

"Well, what does it say?" Torell asked.

"Those who enter this tomb unture of heart will be destroyed and never enter into eternal rest. It also says about the great warrior who was buried here. That he took many surrounding cities and killed many of his enemies. It says that he killed the thieves and traitors to the king and impaled them on spikes as punishment for their evil ways. It also says about how favoured of the king he was in defeating his enemies and was reward with many treasures", told Elrond.

They came to a junction which went left and right. They take the left passage after Roger searched and found no traps in either direction. The passage then turns to the right. John passes a trap which sets off a spear towards him. John quickly used his shield to defend himself. The spear just impacted against his shield and then the spear reset into the wall again.

"Careful where you tread", said Roger.

The passageway turned to the right and there was a skeleton laying on the floor. Gillian saw that the skeleton had a burnt out torch in his hand. Gillian leaned over the skeleton to grab the torch and a scorpion ran out across Gillian's hand and stung him with it's tail. Gillian shook the scorpion off and it it crawled into a crack in the wall.

"Let me see?" Sarah asked Gillian. "It has poisoned you. We need to find some poison balm."

Further down the passageway they came to a door. Samuel's sword crystal started to glow. They entered a large room with a stone carved table at the far end. Two skeletons came to life which were on the floor in a pile of bones. Gillian felt too weak to fight so Sarah and John fought the skeletons. After they had killed the skeletons Sarah searched under the stone table and found some storage jars. In one of them was some poison balm which they used to help mummify their dead. Sarah rubbed the poison balm onto Gillian's hand which drew out the poison into the leaf.

They returned to the passageway and Roger searched for traps.

"There is a pit trap ahead and a spear trap to the right passageway", said Roger.

"Maybe we can use the broken door against that wall to get across the pit", suggested Torell who noticed it just lying there.

They moved the broken door across the pit and walked over safely. They came to a door either side. They entered the left door. It led into a small room with another stone carved table. Sarah noticed more jars under the table and walked towards it. A trap opened beneath her and she held out her spear to bridge the gap to prevent herself falling into it. Her spear snapped and she started to fall. Elrond cast a levitation spell to stop her falling into the pit below. Sarah was saved from falling into a spike pit.

"Thank you Elrond", thanked Sarah.

"I'm just glad your safe", said Elrond.

Sarah searched the jars under the table and found some more poison balm and also found a gold necklace. They left the room and returned to the passageway. They came to a crossroads and Roger checked for traps and found none. Samuel saw a scorpion crawling across the wall and killed it with his sword. They went forward and came to another door. They entered it and it was dark inside.

Elrond lit Gillian's torch with a fire spell so he could see inside. Samuel's sword crystal started to glow. There was a tomb and the tomb slide open and a mummy wrapped in bandages stood up and started to walk towards Gillian. Gillian threw the torch at the mummy and it burst into flames. The room became dark again after the flames died out after burning the mummy. Elrond cast a light spell and his orb started to glow lighting up the room. Torell searched the tomb and found nothing but lose mummy bandages. Torell pushed the tomb as he leaned on it to get up. The tomb slide across to reveal a hidden switch under it. Roger walked into the passageway and shouted to Torell to press the switch. A wall slide to one side showing some stairs leading down.

"That's it Torell, you have found a way down", said Roger.

They all headed down into the next level of the pyramid. They came to a crossroads inside the pyramid and Roger checked ahead.

"There is a large pit ahead that is too long to get across", reported Roger.

"What about the passage to the left or the right?" Samuel asked.

"Both are clear of any traps", replied Roger.

"Let us try the left path first", said Samuel.

The passage turned right and the passage came to an end with a door to the right wall. Samuel's sword crystal started to glow again. They entered the room to find a mummy wandering around a large room. As soon as it saw them enter the room it leapt towards them with it's arms outstretched. Samuel slashed his sword at the mummy cutting it's arms off. The mummy backed away and Samuel stabbed the mummy through it's chest and the mummy turned to dust on the floor. They searched the room afterwards. Torell found a switch on the floor and pressed it down with his foot.

"Let's try the passage forward now to see if the pit has gone", said Samuel.

They went back to the passageway that went forward. The pit trap had gone and a raised stone walkway had replaced it so they could cross. John crossed over the walkway first and the others followed. John walked up further and set of a spear trap. John shielded himself from the spear that shot out from the side of the wall.

"Stay back, there are more traps", said John.

"Maybe there is a switch on the right passage, you stay here and we will go back to try and disarm the traps", said Roger.

All but John went back to the right passage. It turned left and they entered a large room the same as on the other side. Samuel's sword crystal started to glow.

"Becareful it could be another mummy", warned Samuel.

A mummy came out to attack and Torell was ready with an arrow already aimed expecting to find another mummy. He fired and it hit straight into it's chest killing the mummy and turning it into dust. Roger found a switch and pressed it deactivating the spear traps along the passageway where John was waiting. They returned to where John was waiting for them. They continue down the passageway until it turned to the left. They came to a door and Gillian, Torell and Elrond entered it. A skeleton was sitting on a golden throne. As Gillian neared the throne the skeleton came to life and drew his sword. Gillian fought with the skeleton and after a few blows killed it. Gillian felt tired and rested on the throne. Gillian felt some magical power surge through the throne and he felt his energy restored and felt stronger.

"What just happened to me, I fell stronger", said Gillian.

Elrond took a look at the throne and used an understanding spell to read the hieroglyphs, "It says: Who may sit on this throne may be given life, health and strength for all eternity."

"So if I stay on this throne I would live forever?" Gillian asked.

"Yes but you would end up like that skeleton never being able to leave the throne", said Elrond.

They returned to the others who were looking down a pit with spikes at the bottom.

"We have to jump across it, there is no other way forward", said Roger. Gillian leant against a wall and the wall moved slightly.

"Gillian, I think you have found a secret door", said Sarah.

Gillian pushed it. It was very heavy but with his new found strength from the magical throne he could push it open. They entered a small room with a door that led back into the corridor the other side of the spiked pit trap.

The path twisted round to the right through a narrow passageway with a high ceiling. There was a blue stone door to their left. Elrond used his magic to try and open the door but it was closed by a stronger magic. They continued on and the passageway twisted left and then right until they came to a red door on the right. Sarah leaned against the left wall and stepped on a switch which opened a stone door behind her. Sarah fell through the doorway into the room and the stone door fell closed again. Gillian tried to lift the stone door but it was too heavy.

"I can't lift it. It's too heavy. My magical strength must have worn off", said Gillian.

Sarah was trapped inside the room and couldn't open the stone door as it had slid firmly down into the floor. Sarah looked around and saw a coffin and a wall with a weapons rack on it. The coffin opened and a mummy stood up with long flowing bandages lose from it's arms. Sarah grabbed a sword from the weapons rack to defend herself. The mummy used the lose bandages from its arms like whips to hit Sarah. Sarah dodged left then right to avoid the hits from the mummy. The mummy groaned as if in pain and tried to hit Sarah again. The mummy attacked whipping one of it's long bandages from it's arms. The bandage rapped around Sarah's sword. The mummy pulled the sword away from Sarah's hand and threw it across the room out of Sarah's reach. The mummy attacked again at Sarah. She rolled across the floor and grabbed a spear from the weapons rack. The mummy tried to hit Sarah again and Sarah dodged to the right and then threw the spear at the mummy. It hit the mummy in it's chest and it exploded into dust. Sarah went over to the coffin and found a gold ring inside and put the gold ring into her bag and she picked up the spear to replace her broken one that she had lost earlier. Sarah then searched the room for a switch and found one. Sarah pressed it to open the stone door. As the door opened she rejoined the others in the passageway.

"Are you okay Sarah?" John asked.

"Yes, I stumbled across another mummies tomb and fought him off with this spear I found inside", explained Sarah.

Samuel used the red key to open the door and they all entered a large stone room. Samuel's sword crystal started to glow to warn of danger in the room ahead. Inisde the stone room four mummies stood armed with spears two on either side of the room and one mummy warrior stood at the back of the room near a coffin armed with a sickle sword in one hand and an axe in the other. He wore on his head a scorpion crown and a gold collar around his neck and gold bracelets on his wrists.

Sarah attacked one of the spear mummies and John attacked one of the other spear mummies with the help of Gillian. Roger and Torell took aim and fired at the warrior mummy from behind a broken pillar. The mummy cut the arrows in two with his sickle sword. The warrior mummy leapt towards Torell and wounded his arm with his sickle sword. Samuel attacked the warrior mummy. The warrior mummy wounded Samuel's arm with his axe and Samuel dropped his sword. The warrior mummy raised his sickle sword high into the air to finish Samuel off when Gillian and John joined in the battle. Elrond used his magic to fire a fireball at one of the mummies armed with a spear killing it. Sarah killed the other mummy by stabbing it in his chest and it turned to dust on the floor. Gillian cut off the warriors mummies arm holding the axe. The warrior mummy backed away and Elrond threw another fireball this time at the warrior mummy. It missed and hit the wall. Roger fired at the mummy and the arrow hit the mummies gold collar and bounced off. Samuel had picked up his sword by this time and attacked the warrior mummy. As Samuel attacked the mummy one of his blows hit his gold bracelet as it defended itself. Samuel pushed the mummy away and it fell back onto the coffin. Samuel raised his sword and stabled the mummy in the chest. The warrior mummy burst into dust.

Samuel took the gold collar from the dead warrior mummy and his two gold wrist bracelets. Samuel opened the coffin and found a blue key. "We now have two keys to the Seven Towers, we just need to find the other five."

They headed back to the blue stone door. Samuel used the blue key and the magic that sealed the door shut disappeared. Inside was a chest guarded by a cobra. Roger took aim and fired an arrow killing the cobra. Samuel opened the chest to find some scale armour. It was tougher than his plate armour and he put it on and gave his plate armour to Torell. Sarah bandaged Samuel and Torell's wounds with fresh bandages from her bag and used her heal magic to help heal their wounds. They exited from the pyramid the same way they came in.

They set off towards the city Theb. They travel north out of the desert and camped by the river. They eat that night wild boar that Roger and Torell help capture and ate with it dried apricots and nuts. The next morning they make some soup from the bones and tail of the boar and some dried tomatoes. They set off again north towards the city Theb. They passed under Elf Wood and crossed over a wooden bridge to reach the city Theb. Sarah showed Elrond the ring she found in a coffin inside the tomb of the pyramid. Elrond uses a spell to read the markings on the ring.

"It says that with this ring the gods will protect you", said Elrond.

Sarah puts the gold ring on her finger for protection.

When they arrived at the city of Theb Sarah took the gold necklace that she found and sold it in a jeweller's shop for 80 gold. Samuel sells the gold collar he took from the warrior mummy in the same jeweller's shop for 100 gold.

With the money Sarah bought some gown mail. Gillian bought some chain mail. Samuel saw the gold helmet the thief took from the pyramid that he sold to the shop. The same man that sold him the map to the pyramid's secret entrance. The price was two hundred and fifty gold crowns. The man in the shop said it was of the finest quality for a helmet he had ever seen. Samuel wish he had the money to by it, but only had enough money left to buy food and lodges for his friends.

They all eat at the tavern and lodge for the night which costs them 60 gold crowns in a tavern called the King's Crown. The next day Samuel, Roger and Gillian venture outside and wander around the city. A town crier shouts out some news, "Hear ye, hear ye. King's crown has been stolen, reward given. Hear ye, hear ye."

Samuel talks to the town crier. "Excuse me, you said something about the king's crown being stolen and a reward?"

"Yes, two hundred gold crowns as a reward if anyone finds and returns the king's crown. It has been said that thugs and thieves stole the king's crown from his storeroom home and fled to the lonely mountains. Some have gone looking for the crown but have never returned. Some say that the mountains are cursed or enchanted by evil magic but others say they have been killed and captured by the band of thugs", answered the town crier.

"Gillian and Roger, do you think we could find that crown in the lonely mountains?" Samuel asked.

"Well, we have killed goblins and witches before. A band of thugs should be no different", said Gillian.

They return to the tavern called the King's Crown and tell the others of their next quest.

"We have heard of a reward to find and return the king's crown that has been stolen", said Samuel to his friends in the tavern.

"Funny how this tavern is called the King's Crown, what a coincidence", said Torell.

"We need some money to help in our quest. We are little short of money and we need to buy better weapons and armour if we are going to take on more difficult enemies", said Samuel.

"Yes, your right, but where are we going to start to look for this crown?" Elrond asked.

"I have heard the thugs that stole the crown are hiding out in the lonely mountains", said Samuel.

"The lonely mountains. I have heard stories of an evil witch that cursed the mountain so no traveller could pass through the mountains. I guess she wanted to keep people away and that is why they call them the lonely mountains", said Elrond.

"We have fought with a witch before, this one should be no different", said Samuel.

"I think we can do it and we could do with that reward", said Elrond.

They all set off that morning towards the lonely mountains. Elrond picks some bane root from the woods outside the City of Theb, and finds three of them and then puts them in his bag. They then crossed over Wooden Bridge and headed north into the lonely mountains. They start to climb up the rocky path over the mountains. After reaching the top of the mountains they walk over a narrow path through the tops of the mountains. The green valley disappears below covered by mist and they can see the mountain drop down either side of the rocky mountain path. They go down where one of the mountains flatten out to reveal a plain of sharp pointed rocks. They can see a small hut with smoke coming out from the top of its stone built chimney.

"Do you think that this is where the witch lives or the thugs hideout?" John asked.

"We will soon find out. Ready your weapons", said Samuel.

The evil witch was wearing black and purple and she came out from her hut and shouted, "How dare you intrude on my mountain. You shall be punished."

The witch held up her orb staff with a decorated snake coiled around it and lighting flashed down from the sky and hit six large rocks around them. The rocks creaked and reformed into stone shaped men. They attacked Samuel and his men. Their weapons could not hurt the stone monsters. Gillian swung his sword as hard as he could at one of the stone monsters and managed to cut it's head off. Roger and Torell fired arrow after arrow at the stone monsters which slowed them down and weakened them. Sarah killed one with her spear after much fighting. Samuel killed another and Torell killed one with his bow. John chopped off the head of another and Elrond killed one with a fireball. The broken rocks lay on the ground and then fused back together again to make one giant rock monster. The witch let out a wicked laugh.

"It looks like only magic can kill a creature this big", said Elrond and used one of his scrolls to cast an earthquake spell and uses the bane root he found in the woods earlier to help cast the spell. The earth shook, and a crack opened up in the ground beneath the monster. The stone giant fell down into the ground and parts of it fell apart as it sunk into the ground. Samuel and the others cheered because of Elrond's great magic. The witch looked angry and wasn't to be outdone by a wizard and held her staff into the air again and then smote it against the earth. The sharp rocks broke off into pieces and a strong wind blew towards Samuel and his men. Samuel and John tried to shield the others from the flying shards of rock caught in the wind blowing towards them.

"Get behind us", shouted John.

Three shards of rock hit Elrond and cut his arm. Then as by magic a shield of light fell around them and the witch weakened and her spell stopped.

Gillian took the moment to run towards the witch and attacked her. The witch moved to avoid Gillian's attacks and defended herself with her staff. The witch swung her orb staff to hit Gillian. Gillian dodged the attacked and thrust his sword into the witches chest. The witch fell face down dead onto the ground.

"Elrond that was amazing magic, how did you do a protective shield of light?" Sarah asked.

"It was not me. I don't know where that came from", said Elrond.

Then from behind one of the rocks came an old bearded man, "Hello Elrond."

"It is my old master, the one who taught me magic", said Elrond.

"I was watching you. You did well to defeat that rock giant", said his master.

"What are you doing up here?" Elrond asked.

"That evil witch you killed stole a magic spell book from one of the wizard towers. I came here to get it back, but it looks like you have saved me the trouble of killing her yourself's. And who are these people who travel with you?" The wizard master asked.

"This is my friend Samuel, Gillian, Roger, John, Torell and Sarah. I said I would help them on a quest to get the sword to kill the demon lord", replied Elrond.

"A very noble quest, but also a very dangerous one. Elrond I know I have taught you some spells but there is still much you must learn. Come and visit me at the twin towers in spider wood and I will teach you some more spells. And also you young Sarah I can teach you some magic as well. You are a priestess is that right?" The master wizard asked.

"Yes, that's right, I would like to learn more magic", said Sarah.

"Well, when you get a chance come and visit me at the twin towers and I will teach you both new spells to help you on your quest", said the master wizard. "Now I must go and take the magic book that this evil witch stole from us back."

Samuel and his men moved on through the lonely mountains until they reached the thug camp. The thug camp had huts and a wooden spiked fence surrounding their huts. The thugs had wild looking hair and blackened faces from ash from their camp fires, and wore leather and plate armour on their legs, head and shoulders. The thugs came out of their camp to attack them. There was sixteen of them. Torell and Roger fired arrows at them killing four of them. Gillian, John, Sarah and Samuel killed another one each. Elrond fired a fireball at one of them killing him. The leader of the camp stood still with his remaining men.

He stood in fear and then said, "Wait until my leader finds out what you have done here to his secret camp." Then he turned and fled with his men down the mountain side.

"What do you think there plan was?" Samuel asked Torell.

"If I know thugs and bandits they usually set up camp near to a town or village and steal what ever they can from there. Then they sell what they steal to buy weapons and then attack that city and then afterwards they move onto the next town or village.

"I have found the king's crown", said Roger searching one of the larger huts.

"Well done Roger, now we can go back to the city of Theb and claim our reward", said Samuel.

They returned to the city of Theb and saw the king and returned his crown. The kings daughter sat next to him wearing a white gown.

"Thank you kind sirs for returning my crown. I reward you with two hundred gold coins", said the king of Theb.

"Thank you", said Samuel down on one knee.

"You have been very brave. Many men have tried to return this crown to me and failed. I am very grateful. The city will hold a feast in your honour tonight and you are all welcome to sit and eat at the king's table", said the king.

"Thank you once again", said Samuel.

A feast was held that night and they all sat at the kings table to the left of the king. On the right sat his daughter and the king's nobles and court men. Gillian took advantage of the free food and ate enough brazen boar until he was full. After the feast they returned to the King's Crown tavern to retire to bed. The king of Theb made sure their stay in the King's Crown was for free as thanks for returning his crown.

The next day Samuel and his friends awoke late after the long day of fighting and trekking up the lonely mountains and defeating the witch and the thugs the day before. One of the king's servants came to see Samuel at the tavern. "I have a note from the king, he requests you come urgently to the king's house."

Samuel followed the servant to the king's house.

"What is it your majesty?" Samuel asked.

"I have just received a note from the band of thugs. They have kidnapped my daughter Verona. They left this note", replied the king pacing up and down worried.

Samuel took the note and read it. It read: - Oh king we have taken your daughter. If you want to see her again alive you will give me 2,000 gold on the night that we return with a band of twenty men in two weeks time. If you do not pay my men when they come your daughter will die.

"It looks like they are trying to get us back for returning your crown", said Samuel.

"You must save her Samuel. If not I am lost without my beloved daughter. You can take my horses and rush to save her as fast as you can", said the king.

"Yes I will. Give us a day to get ready and to find out where these thugs might have taken your daughter and we will rescue your daughter tomorrow", said Samuel.

"Thank you", said the king.

"Where did you last see your daughter?" Samuel asked.

"She went out riding in the woods south of here to meet a stranger who she had been hiding from me and she never returned. Her horse was found with this note attached to it's saddle", replied the king.

"I will find her and return her, I promise oh king", said Samuel.

Samuel returned to the tavern.

"We have another quest to do for the king. His daughter has been kidnapped, and we have to find her", said Samuel.

"But how are we going to find her. Those thugs could have taken her anywhere?" John questioned.

"We start by searching the south wood. That was where she was last seen", said Samuel.

A man with a raised hood approached Samuel and said,

"If you want to find out where the princess is meet me on the edge of the wood at midnight tonight." And then the man left.

"Wait!" Samuel shouted and went outside looking for him but he was already gone.

"What was that about?" John asked.

"I think that man might know where the princess is being held. I need to meet him on the edge of south wood at midnight tonight.

That night Samuel, Roger and John went to south wood at midnight. The hooded man was there waiting.

"Do you remember me?" The man said pulling down his hood revealing his face.

"Should I?" Samuel asked.

"I am Jumbo Jack, the man you rescued from the royal prison", answered the man.

"I remember", said Samuel. "What are you doing here?"

"I said I would come to the city of Theb, but I fell in love with the king's daughter Verona. We planned to met in secret in the woods away from the king but when I went to meet her I saw her get kidnapped by a band of thugs. I followed them on my horse from a distance so not to get seen but as I neared their hideout I got spotted and one of the thugs fired an arrow and it hit my leg look", said Jumbo.

"I see. Why didn't you tell the king?" Samuel asked.

"He wouldn't believe a thief and I didn't want him to know I was involved with his daughter. He could throw me into prison or think that I kidnapped her. Anyway, I will show you where their hideout is and I will help you rescue her", said Jumbo.

The next day they visited the king and told him they had found where the thugs might have taken her daughter. The king gave them horses to borrow to help them more quickly on their journey. Sarah already had a horse so did not need to borrow one of the king's horses. They met up with Jumbo just on the edge of Theb Wood who was also ridding on a horse, and set off west across Wooden Bridge pass the stone circle and then south to the mountains where the thug hideout lay. During the first day of their journey they camped near the stone circle.

The following day they travelled south over the mountains until they came to the thug hideout. It had a stone wall surrounding a large square building with a flat roof. They used ropes to climb the rear wall of the castle. Gillian and John took out the guards and moved to the roof. They removed one of the stone tiles to the roof and lowered themselves down into an empty room. Jumbo opened the door and peered into the corridor.

"All clear", said Jumbo.

They saw another two guards coming up the stairs. Torell and Roger took aim while the others hid behind a wall support. Roger and Torell killed both guards with well aimed shots from their bows. They entered another room that led them deeper into the thugs hideout. Thug guards were wearing blue armour and some wore red armour with thick darked spiked hair and plate armour. The thug guards attacked. Elrond cast a fire spell using the magic he regained from his orb staff. Pillars of flames shot up from the floor surrounding three armoured thugs and consumed them in the flames.

"Elrond, your magic is getting even more powerful now", said John.

"As a wizard gains more knowledge and experience, his magic increases", said Elrond.

They go through four rooms and come out into a corridor. Roger and Torell take out a couple of guards in the corridor and then they enter a door which leads into another set of rooms. They fight their way through more thug guards until they come to a large room. There are six guards and their leader was standing over the king's daughter who was tired to a wooden pole. There were two burning fires either side of the captured princess contained in black metal framed baskets.

"Take your filthy hands off her!" Shouted Jumbo.

"That's rich coming from a thief", replied the leader.

"You will pay for this", said Jumbo.

"And who are the friends you brought with you", said the leader.

One of the guards whispered in his leaders ear.

"Arh, so these are the ones that returned the stolen crown and defeated my men in the lonely mountains. Well you must be pretty strong to defeat my guards but you will not get past me", said the Thug leader.

Samuel, John and Jumbo went to attack the thug leader while the others fought the guards. Two of the thug leader's personal guards attacked first John and Jumbo. Jumbo was just armed with a short sword and a dagger. The thug leader attacked Samuel. The thug leader was muscular and had plate armour across his arm and armed with a long sword. He had a shield and red mohawk hair. After killing the guards their leader remained. Jumbo had defeated the thug leader with the help of John and Samuel at his side. Samuel knocked the thug leader's shield away and it landed across the floor.

Jumbo held his sword to the leaders throat.

"I told you that you would pay", said Jumbo.

"Please spare me and I will give the order to my guards to let you go free", said the leader.

"You can't be trusted, your life is mine and you shall die here this day", said Jumbo and stuck his sword into his chest killing the thug leader.

"Let's untie the princess and get out of here fast before more guards come", said Roger.

They untied the princess and fled through the castle being chased by thug guards. They returned to the room by which they had entered the castle and climbed up onto the roof. They fought with the guards on the wall and climbed back down the rear of the castle. Roger and Torell fired their arrows while the others climbed down to safety and then they fled over the mountains back to the stone circle to camp for the night.

"Verona I'm so glad you are safe", said Jumbo.

"I'm glad you and your friends rescued me", said Verona.

"Your father the king also asked to help rescue you. Jumbo here helped us find their hideout. If it wasn't for his help we would not have known where to look", said Samuel.

"Does my father know about Jumbo?" Verona asked.

"No, he does not know", said Samuel.

"That is good", replied Verona. "I'm sure my father will reward you."

"Yes, I'm sure", said Samuel.

"So, how did you venture to the city of Theb, you don't look like traders to me?" Verona asked.

"We are on a quest to find the sword which will kill the demon lord", replied Samuel.

"The demon lord. Wow, that is a difficult quest! I know of a ancient treasure that might help you with your quest. I know of this magic armour hidden in the tombs of Azoff.

The armour has a blue gem stone which protects the wearer from some magic. The thugs captured me because I knew where the secret path to Azoff lay. The tomb lies just south of the mountains of the thugs hideout and they didn't even know how close it was. The only way to find it is to go to the tombs at sunset and the entrance shall be revealed. There is a winged demon statue outside and when the sun sets it casts a beam of light showing the entrance. This secret I have kept for many years on my mothers side and this is why anyone trying to find the entrance has failed to find it", said Verona.

"What do you think Samuel?" John asked.

"With that armour we would have a better fighting chance against evil wizards don't you think Elrond?" Samuel asked.

"Yes I do", replied Elrond.

The next day they returned Verona to the king in the city of Theb. The king rewards them with 500 gold crowns for the safe return of his daughter. Jumbo doesn't go with them and keeps his love affair secret with the king's daughter. Gillian buys a battle axe, John buys a royal sword and a bronze helmet, and Roger buys an elf bow like the one Torell has. The city celebrates with the heroes and the king has another feast in honour of Samuel and his men for the safe return of his daughter.

At the feast John says, "Do you know what Gillian, I could get use to this hero stuff."

"I know what you mean", said Gillian eating some turkey leg.

They stay at the King's Crown for the night for free again because the king makes it so.

The next day they set off towards the tombs of Azoff. The journey takes them almost two days and was south of the mountains near the thugs hideout. They find some stone ruins with the demon statue. They wait for the sun to set so that it will cast a shadow to show the entrance. The sun starts to set and the shadow from the statue marked the entrance. The sun shines a beam of light through the glowing eyes of the statue causing the entrance to magically open.

"There it is, let's go", said Samuel excited.

They enter the tomb by a set of stairs leading down, which leads them to a corridor. The torches lined along the walls were out. Elrond uses a light spell to light the torches. They come to a junction which goes left and right and take the left exit. Roger checks for traps and they continue down the passageway until it turns right. A skeleton lies sitting on the ground. Samuel's sword starts to glow warning of danger.

"Careful, the skeleton could be alive", warned Samuel.

The skeleton sprang to live and went towards John to attack him. John killed the skeleton after a few attacks. John sees a door ahead and enters it.

"Wait!" Torell shouted but it was too late.

"The door has locked behind me", shouted John inside a large room.

"Look for a secret door at the other end of the room", shouted Roger.

John looked around the long room. A circle was in the centre of the room with a crystal ball glowing blue. As John moved closer to it sparks from the crystal started to appear and then a lighting bolt shot out hitting John. Another bolt shot out from the crystal ball and John leapt across the circle to the other side. Once outside the circle John was safe and he had suffered little damage and couple of burns to his hands. John found a wooden chest on the other side of the room and opened it. He found it contained one hundred gold crowns. He put them into his money bag and searched for a secret door. After a few minutes he found one and rejoined the others in the corridor.

"What happened to you?" Gillian asked.

"Some magical crystal ball burnt my hands. I'm not going to be able to hold my sword until it heals", said John.

"I'm sorry I can't help. My magic power is too weak to heal any wounds. If I can find an agate gem stone I can restore some of my magic power, but until then I can't help, sorry", said Sarah.

"Don't worry Sarah, we will protect him", said Samuel.

They continued up the corridor which turned to the right again until it came to another door.

"Let me go first this time", said Torell.

Torel entered the room and a cave claver attacked him. The cave claver scratched his arm. Torell pushed the beast away and drew his bow and fired killing the beast in the chest. The others entered the room afterwards. A table was in the centre of the room.

Gillian searched the table, "I found a grey key."

"See if it's one of the quest keys Samuel?" Roger asked.

Samuel searched the diary quickly flicking through the pages, "No, there is no mention of a grey key"

"Maybe it unlocks something else", said Elrond.

Gillian pocketed the key.

"I think I have found a secret door", said Roger.

Roger pushed it open and a hungry cave claver attacked him. Samuel came to Rogers defence and cut off the arm of the beast and Roger took aim with his bow and finished it off.

"It looks like it was trapped inside this room", said Sarah.

There was a cupboard and Samuel searched inside the cupboard and found a lever and pulled it. As he pulled the lever it made a clicking sound.

"What was that?" Gillian asked.

"I think I found a switch that may have disarmed the traps", said Samuel.

They returned to the corridor and came to a crossroads. To the left a portcullis blocked their path.

Samuel's sword crystal started to glow. A skeleton came towards them just ahead of them and attacked. Elrond used a fireball to destroy it.

They turned to the right and entered a room. The room was empty so they searched for a floor switch to raise the portcullis. Gillian found the floor switch and they could hear the portcullis begin to rise. They returned to the corridor and went down a flight of stairs down to the next level.

They entered the new corridor and it turned to the left. A blob fell from the ceiling onto John's head. The blob then fell on the floor. John panicked and threw his helmet on the floor. The blob moved over to the helmet and melted it like acid. Torell and Roger fired at the blob and their arrows just dissolved into it. Elrond fired a fireball at the acid blob destroying it. They then continued along the corridor until it turned to the left. Another blob fell from the ceiling and Samuel swung his sword through it slicing it in half and the acid blob broke up into small blobs as it hit the ground. They came to another crossroads. To the left there was another portcullis. They continued to go straight ahead. A blob came towards Gillian. Gillian attacked with his sword. He killed the blob but the acid started to eat away at his sword. Gillian threw it on the floor. As they reached the door they could see handles from acid eaten weapons along the corridor. They came to a door and entered. A cave claver was inside and attacked Samuel. Samuel defended with his shield and fought it off and then killed it in the chest. They found a floor switch to open the portcullis and returned to the corridor and went past the portcullis until they came to a door. Samuel's sword crystal started to glow. Sarah entered the room first this time. A skeleton warrior with a shield and armour attacked. Sarah fought against the skeleton with her spear. Gillian used his axe and struck a heavy blow to the skeleton's head piecing its helmet and crushing it s skull. The skeleton fell dead to the floor into a pile of bones. Sarah stood on a switch by luck and they entered the crossroad into the south corridor and past an open portcullis which Sarah opened with the last switch. They came to a junction and to the right was another closed portcullis so they went left. Another blob fell from the ceiling. Elrond fired a fireball killing it. They came to a door at the end of the corridor and entered the room. Another cave claver was inside and Gillian killed it with his axe. Gillian saw a metal chest and found it was locked. He tried the grey key he had found and opened the chest. Inside was a potion. Elrond examined the potion and discovered it was a heal potion. Gillian gave some to Torell and some to John to help heal them. They searched for another switch and found one that opened the last portcullis they had found. They entered the corridor again and entered another room with a cave claver inside. Gillian killed it again and they found another switch to open a portcullis which had blocked their way down to the next level.

"Who ever thought of guarding each portcullis with a switch and a cave claver in each room was pretty clever", said John.

They went down the stairs to the next level. They follow along the corridor until it turned to the left and came to a door. Gillian opens the door and enters the room. A vampire bat swoops down and bites Gillian in the neck.

"Get it off me, get it off me!" Gillian screamed.

Sarah lunged her spear at the bat and it released Gillian's neck and flew into the air. Torell took aim with his bow and fired an arrow killing it.

"Are you okay Gillian?" Elrond asked.

"I feel a bit drained, like I have lost my strength or something.", said Gillian.

Sarah searched the room and found in the corner of the room an agate gem. Sarah used the agate gem to restore some of her lost magic power.

"Let me help", said Sarah and put her hands on Gillian's neck. Her hands glowed blue and healed the wound. "Hows that?"

"Much better now, thank you", thanked Gillian.

There was another door on the left side of the wall. Samuel opened the door and it was dark inside.

Elrond used a light spell and his staff started to glow to light up the room. Roger searched the room and found a scroll of parchment.

"Look what I have found Sarah", said Roger.

"I can read this. It's a shield spell. I can learn the spell so I can use it to protect myself", said Sarah.

They went back into the corridor and followed it along until it turned to the left. They came to a door and John entered first followed by the others. Samuel's sword crystal started to glow. A skeleton warrior wearing rusty metal armour stood in a large room guarding a weapons rack. John and Samuel fought with the skeleton. The skeleton dodged their attacks defending with it's shield and struck back at Samuel. Samuel dodged it's blows and John swung his sword towards the skeletons head slicing it off killing it.

Gillian searched the weapons rack and found amongst the rusty weapons a well perseved barbarians sword. He replaced his long sword which had been eaten by rust from the acid blob with the barbarians sword which he found on the weapons rack.

They returned to the corridor and it came to a dead end. They entered the door at the end of the corridor and entered a dark room. Elrond used a light spell to make his orb staff shine to light up the room. Roger searched the room and found a secret door and entered. He saw a lever on the floor and pulled it.

"What did that do?" Samuel asked.

"Maybe there was an entrance we missed", said Roger.

Torell led them back into the corridor and found a junction they had missed. It led to a corridor ahead that came to a disc shaped room. There was a door on the other side of the room and they entered it. They followed the corridor round to the left which led them to a room and they entered it.

Samuel's sword crystal started to glow. Once inside they saw a large room with two tombs on the ground. Two hyper zombies attacked them. Samuel attacked and attacked but the zombie he was fighting took the blows without much damage. Gillian fought with the other zombie and was having the same trouble. Torell and Roger fired an arrow at them as Gillian and Samuel backed away from them. The zombies glowed purple as they started to heal. Torell fired again and again and after a while managed to kill one while the other attacked Sarah. Sarah finished the hyper zombie off with her spear.

Torell pushed one of the tombs aside and a click was heard and then the sound of gears turning was heard.

"What was that?" Gillian asked.

"Maybe that disc room has moved again", said Roger.

They returned to the disc room and the door on the other side had changed position. Sarah entered the door first followed by the others. Sarah fell into a pit trap and her spear bridged the gap. Sarah swung out of the pit to safety. The others jumped across the pit.

"It's a dead end", said Samuel.

"This can't be it. The treasure must be hidden somewhere", said John.

They searched along the wall and Torell found a secret door. Samuel's sword crystal started to glow. It led them into a large room with two more hyper zombies. Roger and Torell fired arrows at them. As they started to glow purple Gillian and Samuel finished them off. They searched the room again and Sarah found a secret door. Samuel's sword crystal was still glowing warning of danger ahead. They entered a large room. Two armoured ghosts wearing chest armour and spiked helmets, and armed with a staff axe stood guard over a tomb. Sarah, Gillian and Samuel battled one while Elrond used a fireball spell at the other. The fireball hit the armoured ghost but was still alive. John finished it off with his sword. Samuel's sword crystal continued to glow. The tomb opened and a skeleton wearing purple shabby robes and a pointed cone hat stood up. He held his staff up and two green circles of light appeared on the floor. Out of each green circle of light appeared two skeletons armed with a cutlass in it's hand. Gillian and John fought one while Samuel and Sarah fought the other. Torell and Roger fired arrows at the undead wizard. The undead wizard moved swiftly away dodging their arrows. The undead wizard held up his staff and fired a red beam of light at Elrond. Elrond tried to use a fireball spell but couldn't as if he had been cursed by the red beam of light and couldn't use magic spells. The undead wizard knocked Torell to the ground with his staff. Roger took aim with his bow. The undead wizard held out his bony hand towards Roger's chest and sucked his life energy from him. Roger fell weakened like an old man. Elrond fought the undead wizard with his orb staff. The undead wizard knocked Elrond to the floor. Sarah left the skeleton she was fighting to attack the undead wizard. Sarah used the shield spell and a yellow light surrounded her. The undead spells couldn't hurt Sarah any more. Sarah thrust her spear into the undead wizard killing it. The summoned skeletons disappeared and they turned to Roger where he lay.

"Are you okay?" Sarah asked.

"I feel weak", said Roger.

"My magic is too weak to heal you. That shield spell took a lot out of me", said Sarah.

"Don't worry Roger, we will get you back to town so you can rest", said Samuel.

Samuel searched the tomb and found the lighting armour. He gave his scale armour to Roger and put on the lighting armour. The lighting armour glowed blue with magical energy that surrounded it and the energy moved in waves. They left the tombs off Azoff carrying weakened Roger. They headed towards the river and met a group of fishermen who wear repairing their nets by their boat.

"I wonder if you can help us. My friend is injured and we need help in getting him back to the City of Theb. Could you take us there by boat?" Samuel asked.

"Well it's a bit out of our way. We was planning to head south of the river not north, replied the captain of the boat.

"We can pay you fifty gold crowns", said Samuel.

"Okay then, you got yourself's a deal", said the captain of the boat.

They all got into the boat and headed up the river to the city of Theb. They anchored near Wooden Bridge and Samuel paid them fifty gold crowns for their help. They got out of the boat and walked carrying Roger back to the City of Theb. They bought food and lodgings for the night which cost them 60 gold crowns in total.

Chapter 5 – Orcs Lair

The next day the king of the city of Theb hears that Samuel is back in town and requests him to come to his home.

"You wanted to see me oh king" Samuel said.

"Yes, while you was gone an small army of orcs attacked our village. We fought them off but it has left us weakened. I need your help Samuel. I need you to found their lair south of the goblin caves near Orc Retreat. If you bring me back the head of the orc leader I will pay you two hundred gold crowns as a reward. Once the orc leader is killed it will disband the other orcs and cause fighting amongst their tribes and keep us safe from attack. Will you do this for me?" The king asked.

"I will, but can I ask of you one thing", replied Samuel.

"What is that?" The king asked.

"Will you look after Roger for me and keep him rested and feed in the King's Crown tavern for me? He was wounded on our last quest", said Samuel.

"Yes of course. We will take great care of him. I will make sure one of my servants will take care of him", said the king.

"Then the rest of my team accept this quest of yours oh king", said Samuel.

"Thank you, thank you so much", said the king.

Samuel went back to the King's Crown tavern to tell the others of their new quest.

Samuel and his men set out south through the opening between the woods pass the temple of Midus towards the mountains where Orc Retreat was. Their minds were focused on Roger, hoping he would be okay and also worried how they would do their next quest without him.

"What's wrong with you all?" John asked.

"We are worried about Roger are you not worried as well?" Gillian replied.

"He will be well looked after while we are gone", said John.

"How are we going to fight an encampment of orcs with just one archer?" Sarah asked.

"Come on, we have won all our quests so far, we can do this one too, isn't that right Samuel?" John asked.

"Yes, that's right", replied Samuel.

"Just because Roger is wounded doesn't mean we are going to get hurt on this quest, we help one another", said John.

"Your right, we done it before and we can do it again", said Sarah.

As they entered the valley between the mountains a woman dressed in animal skins appeared holding a staff and wore around her neck animal teeth, and a blue stoned bracelet on each of her wrists.

"You can not pass through here travellers, turn back now", warned the woman.

"We need to pass to reach Orc Retreat", said Samuel.

"Ha, ha, har! You must be fools. Why would you risk your lives to enter there?" The woman asked.

"We are on a quest to kill the orc leader who is encamped just beyond these mountains", replied Samuel.

"On a quest hey. Well if that woman there can defeat me in battle then I might consider in letting you pass", said the woman pointing to Sarah.

"Come on Sarah you can do it", said Samuel.

"Be careful this woman is an Amazon woman", whispered Torell to Sarah.

Sarah walked towards the Amazon woman and readied for battle. The Amazon woman walked around Sarah studying her movements. Sarah thrust her spear to attack. Sarah tried the same attack again and then tried again and again. The Amazon dodged each attack. Sarah tried the same attack again and the Amazon woman grabbed her spear and flipped Sarah onto her back. The Amazon woman made an attack at Sarah and Sarah rolled over to avoid the attack and got back onto her feet. Sarah made an overhead attack and the Amazon woman blocked with her staff. Sarah made an attack to the side and the Amazon woman blocked again. The Amazon attacked hitting Sarah on the shoulder. Sarah backed away to think of her next move. Sarah attacked overhead again and the Amazon blocked the attack. Sarah frustrated put down her spear on the floor and grabbed the Amazon woman's staff and flipped her onto her back. Sarah picked up her spear to attack her while she lay on the ground but the Amazon flipped backwards onto her feet and flicked her staff up with her foot into her hand. Sarah had had enough and didn't know what to do next. The Amazon attacked Sarah and Sarah dodged her attack and kicked her in the back causing the Amazon to fall on her face. Sarah held her spear into her back.

"All right, you have won, you may pass", said the Amazon woman disappointed.

Sarah helped her up to her feet, "You fight well, you dodged every attack and I couldn't counter all your attacks, it's just your own attacks are weaker than mine. I have been in training from my clan. I have been on guard duty to prove myself. I feel I have failed them. I will be killed if I return to my village as a I have failed them. May I join you in your quest. I rather die with fools fighting then suffer the humiliation of my tribe."

"Yes you can", said Samuel. "But we are no fools."

"You will have no chance against an encampment of orcs", said the Amazon.

"What about your clan, can they help us get into the encampment. If you bring us to them and tell them our quest maybe they will not be so angry with you", said Sarah.

"I will try, but no man has ever dared enter our camp and lived afterwards", said the Amazon woman.

"We can wait outside your village and you can take Sarah with you, thus respecting your customs", suggested Samuel.

The Amazon led them to the start of the mountain path and told the others to stay there while she brought Sarah with her.

"Samuel do you think Sarah will be all right?" Gillian asked.

"Well Sarah did beat her in battle and didn't hurt her. I think that is trust enough even for an Amazon", replied Samuel.

The Amazon led Sarah to her leader past the huts and ruins of their temple.

"My leader, I have brought this woman who has dared trespass our mountain pass", said the Amazon.

"You have done well Alsta. You have truly proven yourself. Does she want to became one of us?"

The Amazon leader asked.

"No, she is on a quest with some others … men. She is on a quest to the orc encampment", replied Alsta.

"Ha, ha, ha. You make me laugh. No man or woman can enter the orc encampment and live without an army", said the Amazon leader.

"I have joined them and I request the clans help in getting to the orc encampment and once inside we will fight for ourselves", said Alsta.

"I have never seen such bravery. We will help you Alsta and if you choose to join them then that is up to you", said the Amazon leader.

Torell was keeping a look out, "I can see the whole army of Amazons coming."

"Sarah has been killed and they have sent an army to kill us", said John panicky.

"Just wait, we don't know that for sure", said Samuel but he was worried when he saw the whole army of the Amazons.

"I can see Sarah, she is with them", said Torell.

The Amazon leader approached Samuel, "So you are their leader?"

"That's right", replied Samuel.

"You are either brave or stupid or both. Both probably being a man. Anyway you have proved your worth to Alsta and she wishes to join you and I respect her for that, but I can't let her die this day amongst fools. We will help you battle your way into the orc encampment, but after that you are own your own", said the Amazon leader.

"Thank you for your help", said Samuel.

As they entered the orc encampment they could see tents and wooden spiked fences surrounding the orc camp. The Amazon leader made a woo, woo, woo, sound and the other Amazons joined in and moved in to attack. The Amazon archers fired arrows at the orcs. The orcs were taken by surprise and ran and fled. The Amazons fought with swords and spears and defended themselves with wooden shields.

Another group of Amazon women threw their spears and then drew their swords. Some of the orcs stood their ground and fought back with swords to defend their camp.

"We have done our part, now it is up to you", said the Amazon leader.

Samuel led his team into a cave marked by a red orc banner over the entrance and made his way through fighting orcs as he went. The orcs had leather armour and fought with swords. They entered a great hallway supported by wooden posts and orc banners hanged down from the ceiling beams. Ten orcs on each side readied to attack. Elrond used his pillar of flame spell. Three pillars of flame shoot up from the floor engulfing three orcs and killed them. Torell killed two orcs with his bow, and the others fought with their weapons killing more orcs. They came to a gate with two orcs on guard. Samuel and Gillian fought the orcs.

"Close the gate!" An orc shouted.

An orc started to lower the gate. Samuel, Gillian, Sarah, Alsta and John rushed through as the gate started to lower. Torell fired an arrow through the gate killing the orc lowering it but it was too late and the gate closed. More orcs appeared and Elrond fired a fireball killing an orc while Torell fired arrows at others. Samuel and the others moved on leaving Torell and Elrond to fight for themselves. They entered the orc guard room. Six orcs where in the room and took swords to fight from a weapons rack. Alsta defended against an orc but her staff broke. Alsta took a spear from the weapons rack and finished the orc off by stabbing him in the chest. After the orcs where killed they entered another room, it was the orc leaders lair. There was a table each side of the room with a map of orc plans laid on it. At the back of the room sat the orc leader. The orcs overturned the tables to defend themselves by hiding behind them. Two orc warriors armed with shields and chain mail armour defended their leader. Elrond and Torell entered the room.

"What kept you?" Samuel said.

"Orcs what else", replied Torell.

Torell fired arrows but the orcs were hiding behind the tables so were protected. Elrond fired a fireball hitting one of the tables causing it to catch fire. The orcs leapt from behind the burning table and attacked. Torell took one of the orcs out with an arrow. Sarah and Alsta killed another two orcs. Gillian and John fought the orc warriors and Samuel fought the Leader. The leader injured Samuel's sword arm. Gillian after killing the orc warrior attacked the leader with his battle axe and the orc leader defended with his metal shield. Gillian attacked again and the orc leader defended with his shield again but the force from Gillian's attack dented the orc leader's metal shield. Gillian swung his battle axe again knocking the orc leader's shield out of his hand and it slid across the floor. Gillian swung his battle axe again aimed this time at the orc leader's neck and cut the orc leader's head off. Sarah use her heal spell to heal Samuel. Gillian took the head of the orc and put it into a bag to show the king as prove. Samuel took his shield as prove to the king.

"Thank you Alsta for your help and your tribes help in getting us here. Do you want to stay with us?" Samuel asked.

"Yes I do, I want to help you on your quest", said Alsta.

They returned to the king in Theb and showed him the head of the orc leader and his shield.

"Thank you Samuel and your team. With the orc leader killed the other orcs will fight amongst themselves for a new leader. They won't be attacking anyone for a while. Thank you very much. Here is your reward, two hundred gold crown coins", said the king.

Samuel visited Roger in the tavern, "How are you feeling Roger?"

"My wound has healed well but I will not be able to help you on your quest for the moment. I'm not strong enough to use my bow effectively and I will just slow you down", replied Roger.

"Well you can stay in the city of Theb until we pass back to Potters Den, said Samuel.

"Thank you Samuel", said Roger.

"We will take care of you each time we return from a quest", said Samuel.

"I wish I could be coming with you", said Roger.

"Don't worry, you deserve a rest", said Samuel.

With the money from the king as a reward they went to the market the next day. They bought Elrond some gown armour. The gown armour cost 200 gold crowns and used up all their reward money. It had metal plates over the gown for protection.

"Elrond, why do you wizards wear gowns?" Gillian asked.

"Because our magic flows more powerful in gowns. It is all to do with the magic aura that a wizard creates around his body. Normal armour and clothes prevent the magic aura from flowing smoothly around the body and weakens the power of the spell", replied Elrond.

The next day Samuel and his team were hunting in the woods outside the city of Theb when they saw a man dressed in blue, hiding behind the trees.

"Did you see that?" Torell asked.

"It looked like a ninja, you don't often see them around here. I know of a ninja clan that lives in the desert", replied Torell.

"Come out ninja, you have been spotted", said Samuel.

The ninja came out and said, "Shoosh! I'm on a secret mission for my clan. I don't want any one to see me."

"What secret mission?" Samuel asked.

"If you will help me I will tell you but otherwise I can not tell, that is why it is a secret mission", said the blue ninja.

"Okay we can help", agreed Samuel.

"You must tell no one this. I am on a mission from my clan to steal back a magic ninja scroll from the desert ninja clan. I need you to help me get into the inner chamber to steal the scroll", explained the ninja.

"What do we get for helping you?" John asked.

"Inside the castle is a ancient pike staff. It is most valuable and a useful weapon for your Amazon woman or Priestess", said the blue ninja.

"We will help you with your quest", said Samuel.

"Thank you, my name is Samazako", said the Ninja.

They went west into the desert until they came to a medium sized fortress. Black ninjas holding spears and bows where patrolling the four towers of the fortress.

"How are we going to get in there?" John asked.

"Leave that to me", said Samazako.

Samazako threw a grappling hook up the fortress wall. It wedged in between the fortress battlements and he pulled it tight. Samazako climbed the wall and using his skills of stealth sneaked up on one of the guards from behind and killed him. He then dragged the body out of view. Another guard walked his way and Samazako hide behind a wooden box and then fired an arrow at the guard. He hid the body the same as the other. He signalled to the others that it was safe to climb up. Two climbed up at a time.

"The guards will be alerted soon, we must act quickly", said Samazako.

He led them across the fortress battlements until they came to a room with four guards. Samazako threw ninja stars at two guards in the room, killing one and wounding the other. Torell fired an arrow killing one and Samazako finished another off with his sword and Gillian killed another with his battle axe. They continued across the battlements and was fired upon by two guards firing arrows from their bows. Samuel, John and Gillian took cover behind some wooden boxes. Elrond fired a lighting bolt from his hand killing both ninja bowmen at once. They entered the north east tower and Samazako killed a guard with his sword. Another guard who was in the room rung a bell to warn the others in the fortress that they were being attacked.

"I must leave you now to fulfill my mission. Thank you for your help you have helped me distract the guards. Take this map of the fortress and enter this chamber. This is where the ancient pike staff weapon is kept, good luck and may you fight with the strength of dragons and be swift as the wind", said Samazako and leapt over the roof of the fortress and lowered himself down into one of the rooms by a rope.

Samuel followed the map fighting through room after room. Ninjas attacked with swords and some ninjas threw ninja stars. John defend himself with his shield as ninja stars where flung at him. Four ninjas leapt down from a balcony from above and attacked with swords. Alsta threw a ninja onto his back and stabbed him with her spear. Sarah finished another one of with her spear. Torell fired an arrow killing another. Samuel killed the remaining ninja with his sword. They entered a large room and four more ninjas slide down from the roof above on ropes. Torell fired at one of the ninjas as he slid down the rope. Elrond used a fireball to burn the rope. Gillian fought one of them with his battle axe and John killed the other one with his sword. They entered another room. Samuel walked into the room and a dart flew towards him from the wall. Samuel quickly shielded against the dart with his wooden shield. There was no doors showing the way out.

"This better not be a trap to lure us in here", said Samuel seeing no way out.

Sudden a wall swung round and two purple dressed ninjas appeared. They threw ninja stars. John and Samuel defended themselves with their shields. Gillian killed one and Torell shot the other one.

They pushed the wall and it swung round and led them into a large room guarded by four more purple ninjas. On the far wall was the ancient pike staff.

"These ninjas are mine", shouted Alsta. Alsta placed her spear on the ground then flipped kicked one ninja to the ground and then picking up her spear again stabbed him with her spear. Another ninja threw ninja stars at her and she put her spear down and did a backward flip to avoid them. Alsta quickly picked up her spear and killed one and Gillian killed another. Alsta finished the last ninja off and took the pike staff. John searched the dead purple ninjas and found 40 gold crowns.

"Let's get out of here before more come", said Samuel.

"What about Samazako?" John asked.

"He should be okay and anyway I don't know which way he went", replied Samuel.

They went back the way they came dodging the dart trap and back to the battlements the way they came in. They climbed down the rope two by two and ran into the desert as ninja bowmen fired arrows at them from the fortress wall.

Once out of the desert they took some rest and drunk by the river. There they met Samazako.

"I'm glad you got out all right", said Samuel.

"Thank you for helping me once again. I got the scroll that they stole from my clan and can safely return it", said Samazako.

"What scroll is that?" Elrond asked interested.

"It is a spell to help cure poison", said Samazako.

"Could you teach me how it works?" Elrond asked.

"Yes I can but you must promise not to teach another", said Samazako.

"Yes, I promise", said Elrond.

They returned to the edge of the forest and said their goodbyes to Samazako.

"Maybe our path will cross again sometime in the future", said Samazako.

"Maybe", said Samazako.

They returned to the city of Theb and rested at the King's Crown tavern. They checked on Roger and he was up and walking around again.

"You look a lot better", said Samuel.

"Yes, my wound is healing nicely", Said Roger.

That night Samuel checked the dairy to find out where the next key was hidden. He saw a picture of a crystal palace in the ice mountains. The book told of an ice queen who could only be killed by a magic amulet called the amulet of the sun. The ice queen held the silver key. The sun amulet was guarded by a four armed snake demon who live in the desert ruins.

"Tomorrow we continue our quest to get another key. First we need to return south to the desert to get an amulet that can kill the ice queen", said Samuel.

"The ice queen?" Gillian asked.

"She has the silver key and the sun amulet is the only thing that can kill her", said Samuel.

"The sun amulet?" Gillian asked.

"Yes, I have heard of that", said Elrond. "It is said the only thing that can kill the ice queen is a magical sun amulet that was created by a powerful wizard. Do yo now where this amulet is now?"

"I looked in the diary and it says that the sun amulet is guarded by a four armed snake demon in the temple ruins", replied Samuel.

The next day they headed into the desert for what they hoped would be their last time. They met the merchant in the desert and bought some water and an oil flask for a total of 30 gold crowns. The sun was so hot they had to take brakes to drink water and find shade under a palm tree. They reach the ruins and entered into an old fallen down palace. Snakes crawled out from cracks from the stone ruins and crawled across the sandy floor. Elrond used a fireball to kill some of them. Gillian threw an oil flask on the ground and then Torell fired a fire arrow to set the oil alight. The remaining snakes returned to their hiding places within the ruins. Then they entered an old hall with red torn banners. A snake statue stood at the back of the hall. Gillian tried to push it to one side to see if it moved. It moved to the left and revealed a stone stairway leading down. It led into a corridor that went left and right. They took the left path and a beam of light shown through a slit in the ceiling above.

"Wait a moment, something does not seem right here", said Torell.

He fired an arrow that passed through the beam of light and spikes from the floor shot up.

"It's a trap!", exclaimed John.

"We need to find a switch before we can pass that way", said Torell.

They headed to the right path and entered a room with four snake statues within the room. Two on each side facing in. As Samuel started to walk pass the statues, green slime started oozing from the statues mouths covering the floor. Elrond ran towards Samuel dodging the green ooze and Alsta pole vaulted using her spear over the green slime. The others were cut off from them.

"We can't get across?" John said.

"Wait here, we will find a way back", said Samuel.

Samuel, Elrond and Alsta went up some stairs to another room. There was a circle on the floor and as Elrond crossed it he felt his magic drain from his body. A purple glow surrounded Elrond.

"Elrond, what is happening to you?" Samuel asked.

"I felt my magic just drain away. I will not be able to use my magic until I have left this place. It would seem this magic circle is used against wizards to protect this ancient temple from any magic users", said Elrond.

They entered a door that led into another room and searched for a secret door. They found one on the right side of the wall. It led to a corridor and went left and right. They took the left path and found an empty room. Alsta found a switch that deactivated the trap. They then went back into the corridor and took the right path. They followed it until it turned to the right and came to a dead end.

"It's a dead end", said Alsta.

"Maybe it's a false wall", said Elrond.

The three of them pushed against the wall and the wall turned round. They came back to the entrance corridor. They met up with the others waiting there.

"I'm glad you found another way out. We thought you might be trapped", said John.

"Well Elrond ran into a trap of sorts. A magic trap. He can't use any magic until he leaves the temple ruins", said Samuel.

"This place is full of traps and enchantments", said Elrond.

They continued left pass where the spike trap was and went down some more stone steps.

They came to a corridor and two snake men armed with curved swords attacked them. The snake men had a head of a snake and body of a snake with it's tail moving it across the floor but had arms of a man. Gillian attacked with his battle axe and cut one of the snake men in half. The second spat poison in Gillian's face blinding him. Torell fired an arrow killing the second in the chest. Elrond couldn't use his magic to cure the poison from Gillian's eyes as his magic had been drained, so Sarah used her skills to try and get the poison out from his eyes using some poison balm. The poison balm drew out the poison and Gillian was no longer affected by the poison any more.

They came to another corridor to the right and they followed it down until they came to a door. John entered it and was attack by a snake man inside a small room. The snake man spat poison at John. John defended with his knight shield. Sarah then entered the room and stabbed the snake man with her spear through it's back killing it. They entered another small room which was empty and they searched for a secret door. Torell found a secret door which led to a large room. At the far end was a chest. In the centre was a row of spike traps blocking the way to chest. Alsta found a pole lying on the ground and used it to pole vault over the spike traps safely to the other side where the chest was. Inside the chest was a gnome stone. Alsta put the stone inside her bag and pole vaulted back over the spike traps.

"I found this inside", said Alsta showing the others.

"It looks like a gnome stone. It is a magical stone that can teleport you from one place to another. Wizards use it to teleport from one stone ring to another", explained Elrond.

They return back to the corridor and take the left path and enter a long room. Two snake men attack them. Sarah and Alsta use their spears to kill them and then enter another long room. Two more snake men attack and Samuel and John kill them. They enter another corridor which went left and right. They head left until they come to another junction. To the right was a locked blue door. They use the blue key to unlock the door and inside a small room was a chest. Alsta goes to open it and gets a shock from it.

"Ouch! That accursed chest", screams Alsta.

"It is sealed by magic. We can not open it", said Elrond.

They go back to the left path and it turns to the right and they enter through the door. Inside is a large room with four snake men and the four armed snake demon.

"You will never leave thisss plasse alive", hissed the snake demon.

Torell fired arrows at one of the snake men. Alsta and Sarah fought another two, Gillian and Elrond fought the other snake man guard while Samuel and John fought with the snake demon. The snake demon fought Samuel with one side with two swords and John the other side with two swords. It was a long battle of attack and defence. The snake demon spat poison at John. John defended with his shield against the snakes poison spit, but got wounded in his sword arm by one of the snake demon's swords. Samuel fought with the snake demon and was hit in the chest, and was protected by his lighting armour. Sarah killed a snake man and came to Samuel and John's aid. She used a healing spell to help heal John's wounds. Torell killed the snake man he was attacking and took aim at the snake demon. The first arrow stuck him wounding him and as Torell took aim again the snake demon spat poison in his eyes. Torell fell to the floor in pain. Sarah tried to take care of him best she could but she had no more poison balm with her. Gillian attacked the snake demon with his battle axe while Alsta distracted him with her spear. Alsta thrust with her spear and the snake demon defended her blows with his four swords. Gillian went behind the snake demon and swung at the snake demons head slicing it off. The snake demon dropped it's four swords and fell dead on it's front. A crystal key fell to the floor which was around the snake demons neck. Gillian took the key and gave it to Elrond.

"This key must have been magical enchanted to open the magic chest", said Elrond. they went back to the room with the chest inside. Elrond opened the chest with the crystal key to reveal the sun amulet inside.

"This is it", said Elrond holding the disc shaped amulet in the air with a green gem fixed in it's centre.

"We have all we need to kill the ice queen now", said Samuel.

"We better get out of here quick and find a trader with some poison balm before the poison kills Torell", said Sarah.

Torell was still walking but felt weak from the poison. They left the temple ruins and put Torell over Sarah's horse. Then they travelled to the edge of the desert where they found a trader.

"Do you have any poison balm?" Sarah asked the trader.

"No, I'm sorry I don't but I can tell you where to find some. If you travel north on the edge of the Elf Wood, you should find some there", replied the trader.

They headed north towards Elf Wood. Elrond searched the woods and found some poison balm and gave it to Sarah. Sarah used it on Torell to draw out the poison but he was still weak.

"It's no use. We might have saved his life in time but he is still too weak", said Sarah.

"We should take him to his people where they can look after him", suggested John.

They took Torell to Elf Castle. The elves welcomed them and took care of Torell. The elves feed Samuel and his group and they drunk wine. They rested that night in the rooms of the elf castle.

In the morning Samuel saw Torell.

"How are you feeling?" Samuel asked.

"A lot better thank you, but I still feel weak, said Torell.

"It will take a few days for your strength to return", said Samuel.

"I'm sorry I let you down. I wanted to come with you on your quest to the ice queen", said Torell.

"You must rest for now. We will carry on for now without you, but I promise I will return for you and you can continue with us on our quest", said Samuel.

"All right then, but you promise you will come back for me when I am better?" Torell asked.

"Yes, I promise", said Samuel.

Samuel and his friends left Elf Castle.

"We should head towards the ice queen's palace", said Samuel.

"If we use the gnome stone at the stone circle we can travel to the ice queens palace in less time", suggested Elrond.

They journeyed to the stone circle and Elrond met another wizard called Julian.

"Elrond have you heard, that the great wizard's battle spell book has been stolen from the wizards library", said Julian.

"Who would do such a thing?" Elrond asked.

"A wizard seeking power only to destroy the order of the wizards", said Julian.

"Who was guarding the book?" Elrond asked.

"Your former master. And that's another thing, he has disappeared as well", said Julian.

"Do you think he could have stolen the book?" Elrond asked.

"No, because we found his magic staff and spell ingredients as he left them in his room. It was if he was taken as well", said Julian.

"I must find my old master", said Elrond.

"Maybe you should go to the Twin Towers and check his room to find some clues to what happened to him", said Julian.

"Samuel, will you help me find my old master and journey with me to the Twin Towers?" Elrond asked.

"Yes I will. The ice palace can wait, we must help your old master first", said Samuel.

Chapter 6- The Twin Towers

Samuel and his friends headed east to the river south of the city of Theb. Samuel and his friends got a ride on a boat by some fishermen who where heading south to do some fishing along the river south to Spider Wood. The twin towers stood up high above the tree tops of the wood. The two towers were where the wizards and mages trained in magic. Elrond knew of the Twin Towers but had never been there. They entered Spider Wood walking along a path through the trees. Giant black spiders as big as half the size of a human ran out from the bushes. The giant spiders attacked with their long legs and fangs. Gillian stabbed one with his barbarian sword through the giant spider's back killing it. John lopped of the legs of another disabling it. Sarah and Alsta killed another two by spearing them in their side. Green blood run out from the spiders bodies. Three more spiders remained. The spiders ran back and fired webs at Samuel and Elrond. Elrond and Samuel got tangled in their webs and strugled to move. Sarah and Alsta cut them free. John and Gillian killed the remaining spiders. They continued on down the path and spiders came down from the trees on thin threads of silk. Gillian sliced through the thread making a spider drop to the ground. Samuel sliced through another as it hanged from it's thread from one of the trees. John sliced through another and Sarah stabbed one through its body. Elrond used a fireball to burn one of the spiders as it came down from a tree. Three more spiders dropped down from the trees. One of them grabbed Alsta and took her up into the tree tops. Elrond used his lighting magic to kill the spider so not to hurt Alsta. Gillian caught Alsta as she fell.

"Thank you Gillian", said Alsta.

"Anytime", replied Gillian.

"John and Samuel killed the other two spiders.

"Let's run through the woods before we get surrounded by them", said Samuel.

They ran through the woods seeing the odd spider here and there firing their webs at them and running out of bushes. Gillian killed any that came too close to him as he ran.

As they ran they came to a steep bank and slide down it and fell into a giant web that crossed one side of the bank to the other and they all got trapped in the web. There was no spiders to be seen and looking up they could see a blanket of web above them.

Just then an even bigger spider appeared about four times bigger than the others.

"Elrond, do you think you can get us out of this web with a fire spell?" Samuel asked.

"No, it might set the whole web on fire and we all would burn", replied Elrond.

"Can you aim one away from us and aim a fireball spell at that giant spider to give us a bit more time to free us from this web?" Samuel asked.

Elrond fired a fireball aimed at the giant spider. It hit one of its legs and the giant spider backed away. Gillian and Samuel had freed themselves from the web by this time and went to attack the spider. The giant spider flung Samuel back into the web trapping him again. Gillian used his battle axe to cut one of the spiders legs off. The giant spider fired a string of web at Gillian trapping him. Sarah, Alsta and Elrond were now free from the web. Sarah and Alsta thrust their spears at the giant spider and it backed away. Elrond had readied another fireball.

"Wait! don't kill it", shouted a woman mage dressed in purple.

"Why, its trying to kill us?" Alsta questioned.

"It is guarden to these woods. It protects us wizards and mages from outsiders", said the purple mage.

"Can you call it off then?" Elrond asked.

"Freeze spell", the purple mage commanded.

A shower of frost hit the giant spider freezing it in motion.

"Thank you", thanked Elrond.

"I'm surprised a wizard doesn't even know a freeze spell", said the purple mage.

"I'm only a learner and I am searching for my old master", replied Elrond.

"Well, that would explain it. My name is Juliarna", replied the purple mage.

"I am Elrond and these are my friends, Alsta, Samuel, Gillian, Sarah and John", said Elrond.

"So what is your masters name?" Juliarna asked.

"His name is Galafray", answered Elrond.

"The one that was kidnapped by an evil wizard. I knew of him. I will take you to his room. Maybe there you might find a clue of who took him and where", said Juliarna.

Juliarna then took them to the wizards tower.

"Why are there two towers?" Alsta asked.

"One for mages and one for wizards", answered Juliarna.

Juliarna took them to Galafray's room.

"Just call me when you have found something. I will be in the main hall downstairs", said Juliarna

They searched the room. Samuel found a crystal ball inside a small box under a desk wrapped in a cloth.

"What's this?" Samuel asked.

"Let me see?" Elrond asked. "It's a crystal ball. It's usually tired to it's owner. It will show where he is now."

Elrond rubbed the ball and a misty cloud separated inside the ball showing a ruined castle. A wizard was tired to a pole by chains outside some castle ruins.

"Is that your master?' Gillian asked.

"Yes it is", replied Elrond.

"Look! There is a small Island from the river", said John.

Samuel looked at the map looking for an island near the river, "It's not far from here."

"It is very close to the black mountains", said John.

"We should be all right. We will not be needing to go too close to them", said Samuel.

They went to tell Juliarna what they had found and left Galafry's room and met with Juliarna downstairs in the main hall.

"I will come with you. You could do with some help from another magic user if you are going to fight another wizard. Three magic users should be no match against one evil wizard", said Juliarna.

They left the wizards tower and headed to the river.

"Can we get a boat down the river?" John asked.

"No, it's too rocky for a boat and too shallow to go by boat through this part of the river. We must go down the river by raft", said Juliarna.

Gillian used his axe to cut down some trees to use the logs to make a raft. The women made twine to tire the logs together. Those who had armour on took it off and made a net to keep them in. They tied the net to the centre of the raft. Once everyone was on board they set off down the river on the raft.

The evil wizard called "Necromancer" used a crystal ball like the one Elrond had found in Galafry's room and looked into his crystal ball and he could see Samuel and his friends coming up the river on their raft.

"It would seem you have some friends that have come to help you Galafry", said the Necromancer.

"I believe in my apprentice Elrond. He will find a way to stop you", said Galafry.

"With the book of battle magic I think not. Not even you could stop me and now you are my prisoner", said the Necromancer. "We will see how good they are against my magic."

The Necromancer cast a dark red cloud inside his crystal ball and clouds formed overhead over Samuel and his friends. A strong wind blew and the river turned into a ragging torrent.

They steered the raft around the rocks and through the rapids. Lighting struck a tree causing it to fall into the river. They steered around the fallen tree. Lighting struck another tree. Juliarna cast a levitation spell moving the tree out of their way. They passed a narrow pass of rocks and the storm ceased and the water went calm again.

"Thew, we made it!" Samuel exclaimed.

As they entered Death Lake which surrounded the Island a giant serpent sprung up out of the water. The sea serpent dived towards the raft to try to smash it. Gillian steered the raft away from the beasts attack. The sea serpent reared it's head up out of the water for another attack. Alsta attacked the sea serpent with her spear as well as Sarah. Alsta wounded the sea serpent in it's neck and it dived into the sea and then left them alone.

"That was close!" Gillian exclaimed.

They tired their raft to a stake on the Island and put on their armour ready for battle. The Necromancer wore a black hood, black gloves and black trousers. He also wore a grey top which covered the tops of his legs and grey boots. He wore a metal mask to cover his face to hide his true identity. He wore a black belt and a black shoulder strap which held a black large bag to his right side. He had metal arm bracelets on and metal knee capped armour. The Necromancer was angry that they had survived the river and Death Lake's sea serpent. He used a summon spell to summon two harpies. The harpies had wings like a bat and rough skin and leering red eyes. They flew towards Samuel and his team. Sarah and Alsta attacked the harpies with their spears as their weapons were the only weapons that could reach them from a distance as the harpies flapped around them. Gillian swung wildly with his sword. One of the harpies leered at Sarah with it's searing red eyes causing Sarah to go into a trance and stopped her attacking. Alsta speared one in the chest and it fell to the ground dead. Elrond killed the other harpie with a fireball. They continued on to the castle ruins to fight the evil wizard.

"You have done well to get this far but your no match for my magic power", said the Necromancer.

"We shall see", said John boldly.

Gillian, Samuel and John attacked. The Necromancer fired lighting from his fingers hitting all three of them causing them to fall asleep. Next he used a levitation spell to throw rocks at the others. Alsta got hit by one and fell to the ground stunned. Sarah used a shield spell to protect the other magic users. Elrond and Juliarna fired a fireball at the Necromancer. The Necromancer used a shield spell to protect himself.

"Ha, ha, har", the Necromancer laughed. "Even the three of you are not strong enough against my magic."

The Necromancer used an earthquake spell which made them fall to the ground. Juliarna used an anti-magic spell to wake Samuel, John and Gillian up. Then they attacked the Necromancer with their weapons. He defended himself with his skull staff.

The Necromancer used a levitation spell to push Gillian away and then used an earthquake spell to make John and Samuel fall over. Juliarna cast a freeze spell to freeze the Necromancer into ice. Samuel stood up ready to charge at the Necromancer. The Necromancer used a teleportion spell to return to his tower. They untied Galafry.

"He's gone!" John exclaimed.

"To his tower no doubt" said Galafry. "When he saw he was beaten he fled."

"He has got away with the battle book of magic", said Juliarna.

"Yes and that means in time he will become even more powerful", said Galafry.

"Will you help us get that spell book back Samuel?" Juliarna asked.

"I will but first I must go to the crystal palace to destroy the ice queen", replied Samuel.

"Then Elrond I will teach you the freeze spell so you can return safely to the Twin Towers when ever you need to", said Juliarna.

Juliarna taught Elrond the freeze spell.

"Samuel if you are going to battle the ice queen you will need first the sun amulet", said Galafry.

"We already have it", replied Samuel.

"Do you also have the legendary fire sword?" Galafry asked.

"No", replied Samuel.

"You will need it to fight her ice demons or your quest will be too hard. I will show you where to find it. There is a secret cave near the southern mountains. There is a magic symbol on a rock near there. Find the symbol and push it and a hidden wall will open", said Galafry.

"Thank you", thanked Samuel.

"Thank you for your team rescuing me", replied Galafry.

Sarah healed Alsta with a healing spell. Then they all headed back to the Twin Towers. They ate until they were all full and rested the night in the wizards tower.

The next morning they bought some food supplies for their journey ahead. They headed west towards the southern mountains leaving Galafry and Juliarna behind. Juliarna said she would help them when they would try to recover the stolen battle book of spells from the Necromancer.

They found the mountain that Galafry had explained to them, but there was no symbol to be found on the rocks. Elrond used a spell of understanding and the symbol appeared in the rock. Elrond hit the symbol with his orb staff and a secret entrance appeared in the rock which lead down.

As they went down the pathway the path went left and right. They went left and Elrond fell into a pit trap. His staff bridged the gap and Gillian and John helped him out of the pit. They jumped over the pit trap and then they came to a path that went right and then it came to a junction. They went left at the junction rather than going on straight. Samuel searched for any traps. Samuel found another pit trap. They all jumped across the trap. They came to another junction that went left and right. They went right and was attacked by two blobs that dropped down from the ceiling. John and Gillian killed them with ease. Then they came to a door on the left wall. It was locked and they tried the red key to open it but it didn't open, they tried the blue key and that didn't open it either. Elrond used an open door spell and the door opened.

"It must have been sealed with magic", suggested Elrond.

Inside was a small room with a chest inside. The chest was locked and Gillian used his grey key to open the locked chest. There was a hundred gold crowns inside. Gillian took the gold coins and then re-entered the passageway. The passageway continued and then turned left. There was a door on the right wall. They entered a small empty room. Alsta searched the empty room and found a floor switch. She pressed it and they could hear a chain pulling like a gate being raised. They returned to the passageway until it turned right into a dead end. Two more blobs fell from the ceiling and

Sarah and Alsta finished them off. They went back to the previous junction and took the left path. Elrond walked forward and floor spikes sprang up from the floor. Alsta pulled Elrond back quickly to prevent him being hurt by the floor spikes. Alsta jumped over the the spike trap and then the others did the same. The path turned right and came to a large cavern.

A wooden bridge led across a pool of water that filled the cavern below. As they started to cross the bridge, jellyfish leapt from either side of the bridge from the water. Gillian, John and Samuel killed three. Four more leapt from the water. Elrond, Sarah and Alsta killed them. Then a giant jelly fish came up from the water. It's stinging tentacles wrapped around Sarah. Gillian sliced off the tentacle releasing Sarah. John sliced through the giant Jelly fish and it split into two and fell into the water. Gillian picked up Sarah and they ran out of the cavern. Elrond used a cure poison spell to cure Sarah of the stinging tentacles from the giant jellyfish.

They came to a passageway that turned right and then left and then right again. As John walked along the passageway a spear shot out from the wall. John used his knight shield to defend himself. As they continued another spear shot out from the wall. Samuel defended against it with his wooden shield. His wooden shield split from the damage and Samuel left his broken shield on the floor. The path then turned left and there was a portcullis already open.

They went under the portcullis gate and down some stairs deeper into the cave. Another portcullis block the way forward so they searched until they found a secret door. To their surprise they found two secret doors. One on the left and one on the right. Samuel, John and Gillian searched the room on their left and found nothing. Alsta, Elrond and Sarah searched the room on their right. They found a switch to open the portcullis in the passageway. They came to a junction that went left and right. They searched for traps and found none and went left. An orc attacked Gillian in the passageway. Gillian killed the orc with his axe. Gillian searched the orc and found twenty gold coins. The passageway turned right and had two doors along the left wall and another orc stood on guard by another portcullis halfway down the passage. John killed the orc and found another twenty gold coins.

They entered the first door which led into a small room with a table inside. On the table was some thick rope. Elrond took the rope and then they left the room. They walked around the passageway searching each room they came to and found nothing. The passageway led them completely round in a square shape. They passed two more closed portcullises and two empty rooms.

"This could take us ages to find out how to open all these portcullises", said John.

"There must be some more secret rooms", said Elrond.

They started to search along each passageway wall to find a secret door. They found one on the north side wall and searched the small room for a switch to open one of the portcullises. Elrond found a leaver and pulled it and the portcullis on the east side opened. Three orcs came out from behind the gate to attack. Alsta, John and Samuel killed all of the orcs. They searched the orcs and found sixty gold coins between the dead orc bodies. They continued down the long corridor until they came to a door. Inside was a small room with another switch inside. This switch opened the portcullis on the west side.

"One more gate open, one more switch to find to open the last", said Samuel.

"At last, we are almost there", said John.

They entered the gate on the west side and followed down the corridor. They fought two more orcs who were in the corridor and found forty more gold on their bodies. The corridor turned left and there were two doors in left wall. They entered the first door which led into a long room. Four orcs and an orc wearing armour stood at the rear of the room. The orc in armour seemed to be their leader and gave them orders to attack.

Sarah and Alsta attacked the first two orcs with their spears. Elrond used a lighting spell to attack the other two orcs killing them. The orc leader fought Samuel and Gillian, while John helped Sarah and Alsta. Gillian killed the orc leader and searched his body. Gillian found a bronze helmet and 20 gold. Gillian tried on the bronze helmet and it fitted him and he kept it on for protection. John searched the dead orcs and found 60 more gold. At the rear of the room was a small chest. It was locked and Gillian used his grey key to open it. Inside was fifty gold coins. Gillian took the gold.

They then left the room and went into the next door. They entered a small room. They found a pit with someone shouting at the bottom for help.

"Hold on, we will get you out", said Samuel.

John helped pull him out using the rope that Elrond found.

"Thanks for that. Don't know how long I was down there for. You lose all track of time in the darkness", said the man.

"Who did this to you?" Sarah asked.

"Those nasty orcs that's who. I entered their lair from a hole in the top of the cave and they caught me and put me down this dirty old pit. I guess I should be thankful they didn't kill me. Well, I'd better be going now, because I don't want to get caught by those nasty orcs again. Could I use this rope to get back out again?" The man asked.

"Yes, sure", said Elrond passing him the rope.

"Here, for your help take this, they are no good to me these magic stones", said the man and gave Elrond an agate gem stone.

"Thank you", said Elrond taking the agate gem.

"See you laters", said the man and disappeared into the distance.

"Now let us find the switch to the last portcullis", said John.

They searched the other side of the wall and found a secret door. It led them into a large empty room. They searched for a hidden switch and found one on the floor that opened the last portcullis.

They headed to the north portcullis and entered into a corridor. It turned left, then right and then left again.

"There doesn't seem to be any orcs around here", said Sarah.

"It would seem the orcs are too scared to enter this part of the dungeon", said Elrond.

They came to a red door. It was locked. Samuel tried the red key and it opened. It led them into a large room with a magic circle tiled on the floor with three stone statues on either side of the room.

They crossed the magic circle on the floor first by Elrond and then followed by the others. The statues on either side came to life and started to attack them. Elrond defended against one of the statues stone fists with his orb staff. John defended with his shield and fought back with his sword.

Gillian used his battle axe and sliced one in half with an overhead attack. Sarah and Alsta fought the best they could against the stone statues. Samuel managed to slice one of the statues heads off and it fell into pieces on the floor. Elrond used an earthquake spell and used some bane root to cast the spell to destroy the other four. Sarah searched the wall at the end and found a secret door. They entered the room found by Sarah. They entered a small room and there stood a giant rock guarden standing by the door motionless.

"Be careful Samuel", warned Elrond.

"It's not moving though", replied Samuel as he approached the giant stone guarden.

As Samuel moved closer, the statue came to life and struck out at Samuel. It knocked Samuel to the ground. The guarden statue made another attack with it's large fists and Samuel crawled back out of its way. Gillian moved forward to attack the giant guarden statue. His battle axe just scratched the surface of the giant guarden statue. The statue picked up Alsta and Sarah by their spears and threw them across the floor. Elrond used a freeze spell against the statue guarden. The statue guarden was unaffected by the spell.

"How can we stop that thing?" John asked.

"I don't know", said Elrond.

"Well we need to think of something fast or it's going to kill us all", said Samuel.

"Elrond can you use your earthquake again?" Sarah asked.

"I am low on magic power", said Elrond.

"What about the agate gem?" Sarah asked.

"Oh yes, I forgot about that", said Elrond. Elrond used the agate gem to regain some of his magic power. Elrond cast an earthquake spell and used bane root as an ingredient to cast the spell. Elrond aimed the earthquake directly at the statue guarden by throwing the bane root on the ground in front of him and chanting the earthquake spell. The ground began to split in front of Elrond as he tapped his orb staff on the ground as he chanted the spell. The statue guarden began to shake. The pillars in the room started to crack and the ceiling support beams started to fall and fell on top of the statue guarden.

"Take cover!" Elrond shouted.

The statue guarden was trapped and could not move. They walked around it and entered the door. It led them to a small room and at the rear of room was a stone stand with a stone hand holding a sword. The swords blade glowed between yellow and white, and flames darted around the blade.

"It's the legendary flame sword", said John in amazement. "It's true then."

"Not many have ventured this far and survived I doubt", said Elrond.

"John, take the sword", said Samuel.

"You sure you don't want it for yourself?" John asked.

"No, you take it, I have this sword and I think I will still need it to warn me off undead monsters", replied Samuel.

"As you wish", said John. John took the sword carefully but still burnt himself when he got hold of it.

"Ouch!" John dropped the sword on the floor. The swords flame went out. When John picked up the sword again the flames grew around the blade as before.

"It's as if the sword burns from the uses heart", said Elrond.

"Let's leave this place and return to Elf Castle", said Samuel.

They returned to Elf Castle and met Torell again.

"Torell, your looking well", said Samuel.

"My wounds have healed. I am ready to fight with you once again", said Torell.

"That is good, we need all the help we can against the ice queen", said Samuel.

"Come let us eat, you must be hungry from your journey", said Torell.

They ate and told Torell all that had happened since he was away.

"So Samuel how do we get to the ice queens crystal palace?" Gillian asked.

According to the map the mountains surround the ice palace. No one can get there over than crossing the mountains", said Samuel.

"It sounds dangerous", said Elrond.

"Is there any other way to reach the crystal palace?" Sarah asked.

"The diary says there is a stone circle within the mountains. If we use the gnome stone that Alsta has we can teleport from one stone circle to another into the mountains", explained Samuel.

They slept that night in Elf Castle and in the morning they prepared for the journey ahead. With the money from the orcs lair they bought a breast plate for Gillian, a small metal shield for Samuel, leather armour for Alsta and some thick cloaks for all of them to protect them against the cold, for when they travel to the ice queens crystal palace.

Chapter 7 - The Crystal Palace

They took some food provisions given to them by the elves. Then they headed south west to the stone circle.

"Elrond do you know how the gnome stone works? The journal says you need to use a spell to make the gnome stone work" Samuel asked.

"Yes, everyone move inside the stone circle. Alsta, you stand at the centre of the circle holding the gnome stone up in the air. I will use the teleportion spell", said Elrond. They took their places within the stone circle and Alsta held up the gnome stone in the centre. Elrond chanted the teleportion spell; "Elrond, Celrond, Bellaga."

A beam of green light flooded the stones that shot out from the gnome stone and when the light disappeared they found themselves inside a stone circle within a range of snow covered mountains. Snow covered the ground and snow drifted in the wind in small gusts. They wrapped their thick cloaks around them tightly to protect themselves from the cold winds and headed towards the crystal palace.

"Samuel, do you know where you are going?" John asked.

"Yes, it's just north of here. We just need to pass round the bottom of this mountain range", answered Samuel holding the map tightly taking a quick look at it every now and then.

As they passed the mountain range they could see the sharp crystal towers that stood on top of the crystal palace. It flickered blue against the reflection of the sun and against the snow. A crystal wall extended on each side of the crystal palace.

"I doubt many people have seen this",said John.

"I doubt many people have been brave enough to even want to" said Sarah.

"Who would even want to come out to this kind of cold, deserted place", commented Alsta.

"According to the map and the dairy this is where the silver key is kept. Once we have that we will be well on our way to getting most of the keys to enter the Seventh Tower, and then we can get the magical sword to kill the demon lord. I think we have everything we need to defeat this ice queen", said Samuel.

As they walked up to the entrance to the crystal palace they looked up at its high crystal walls and towers above.

"Are you all ready?" Samuel asked everyone.

"As ready as I will ever be", said John.

"Let's do it", said Gillian.

They entered under a portcullis that was already raised. The portcullis was black with sharp spikes sticking out below it. Ice covered the portcullis and icicles hanged from it. There was no fear of keeping the portcullis shut as those who dwelt inside did not fear the outside world and knew that no one would ever approach the crystal palace. Once inside they saw ice covering the floor in the corners because of the cold and large icicles hang from the ceiling. The floor had crystal blue tiles. The hall had three arches, one to the north, one to the east and the other to the west. The north arch and the east arch had a portcullis closed blocking their way in those directions. They entered the west arch altogether which led down a corridor. Two female ice demons approached them with pale blue skin and screamed as they saw them. Torell drew his bow in readiness. One of the ice demons cast an freeze spell at John. John defended with his shield. The ice blast froze against his shield as it impacted casting brake away icicles on the floor that shattered as they hit the ground. Torell fired an arrow from his bow killing one of the female ice demons through her stomach. The other ice demon cast another freeze spell aimed at Gillian. It hit Gillian impacting against his breast plate armour and he was unharmed. Elround cast a freeze spell in return hitting the female ice demon and it froze her solid in ice. Gillian swung his sword at the frozen ice demon shattering it into two onto the floor. They continued onward and entered another room. The floor was frozen and pits lined either side of the room. Elrond slipped on the icy floor and slid towards an open pit. Samuel grabbed hold of Elronds staff to pull him away from the pit.

"Thanks Samuel", thanked Elrond.

"Your welcome, we need you", joked Samuel.

They carefully crossed the room slowly in the middle trying their best not to slip over on the icy floor.

They exited the room and came to another corridor. Two more female ice demons attacked casting ice shards towards them. Alsta dodge the first attack. Sarah got hit by the second cutting her left arm. John used his fire sword by holding it out in front of him and the sword glowed and fired a bolt of flame out towards one of the ice demons covering her in flames and she turn to black ash on the ground. The other female ice demon fired another ice shard at Samuel. Samuel defended with his shield. Alsta then leapt towards the ice demon and stabbed her spear through it's stomach finishing it off. They entered another room at the end of the corridor with four female ice demons inside with a small frosted chest at the rear of the room to the right side.

Torell quickly took aim and killed one of the ice demons. An ice demon fired a freeze spell hitting Gillian freezing him solid as it hit him. Elrond cast a freeze spell hitting one of the ice demons. John finished the frozen ice demon off with his sword. Alsta killed another ice demon. The remaining ice demon attacked Alsta with her sharp spike arm wounding Alsta's arm. John used his fire sword and fired a fire blast from it to finish the remaining one off. Sarah used a heal wound spell on herself and then on Alsta.

"Thanks Sarah", thanked Alsta.

Torell used an anti-magic unfreeze spell to release Gillian.

"Thank you for freeing me", thanked Gillian.

"I didn't know elf's knew magic?" Elrond asked.

"Yes, but very little. Our people once was taught by a wandering wizard. He taught our people special spells to cancel magic that could be used against our people. It was taught so we could protect ourselves from evil wizards. That spell has been passed down from one elect warrior to another. While I recovered, an elder elf taught me this spell after I told him about my quest with you Samuel", explained Torell.

Gillian used his grey key to unlock the chest. Gillian found a ring inside the chest and handed it to Elrond to have a look.

"This appears to be a magic ring that increases a wizards magic power", said Elrond. "Can I keep it Gillian?"

"Yea sure, I have no use for a magic ring", replied Gillian.

The door at the end of the room led to another corridor with two more ice demons. John and Torell killed them and they continued onward. The corridor went left and right. They went left and Alsta fell into a pit trap. Alsta hurt her foot as she fell. Elrond helped pull her up.

"I can't go on, I have hurt my foot. I will only slow you down", said Alsta.

"I will stay with you to protect you", said Gillian.

"Are you sure?" Samuel asked.

"Yes, go on with out me. Gillian will protect me if that is alll right with him", said Alsta.

"Yes, I will stay here to protect her", said Gillian.

The rest of them went right and came to another room. Ice covered the floor and the air felt icy and cold. As they started to cross the floor spikes shot up from the ground. John pulled Samuel back so that he didn't get hurt by the floor spikes.

"How are we going to cross to the other side?" Samuel asked.

"Maybe there's a secret door or something", said Torell.

They each searched the wall nearest them and Samuel found a secret door that led to a small room. In the small room was a helmet resting on a post. As Samuel took the helmet from it's resting post a portcullis closed off the exit across the room.

"No we can't exit the room", said John in despair.

"There must be an answer to this", thought Samuel.

Samuel place the helmet back on the post. The portcullis raised again.

"We can't take the helmet with us then", said John.

"Yes but we can't cross the floor because of the floor spikes", said Elrond.

"Wait a moment, I have an idea", Samuel put on the helmet and looked across the room. The floor glowed green where the floor spikes lay. "Follow my steps carefully."

Samuel led them safely across the floor wearing the helmet. Once across he placed the helmet on a post on the other side of the room and the portcullis opened. They entered another corridor that turned left and then right. They fought with another couple of female ice demons. Sarah killed one with her spear and Elrond fired a fireball killing the other one. The corridor turned to the right and they entered a small room. A female ice demon attacked firing shards of ice at them. Samuel and John defended against the ice blasts with their shields. John fired a blast from his fire sword killing the ice demon turning her to ash. There was a leaver frozen next to the wall. John tried to pull it but it didn't move. Samuel tried next and couldn't move the leaver.

"It's no use, it will not move", said Samuel.

"John try a fire blast from the fire sword to try to unfreeze it", suggested Elrond.

John fired an ice blast and the ice covering the leaver melted. John then tried to pull the leaver and the leaver moved and a clanking of a chain was heard in the distance.

"Maybe one of the gates have opened", said Samuel.

They returned to were Gillian and Alsta was waiting for them.

"Gillian can you carry Alsta back to the entrance hall and wait there for us?" Samuel asked.

"Yes, if Alsta does not mind me carrying her", said Gillian.

"Only this once, I am not used to a man helping me, but I will make an exception because I am hurt", said Alsta.

They returned to the main entrance and the portcullis in the north archway was open. They went forward into a corridor and two female ice demons attacked them. One fired a freeze blast at Samuel. Samuel defended with his shield and his lighting armour protected him from being frozen. Torell fired an arrow from his bow killing one ice demon and John fired a fireball from his sword killing the other one. They entered a long hall with four female ice demons inside. Torell took aim quickly killing one before it could attack. One of the female ice demons fired a freeze blast and froze John before he could defend. Sarah attacked a female ice demon killing it. Another ice demon fired ice shards towards Elrond and Sarah. Sarah cast a sheild spell to protect them. Torell unfroze John with an anti-magic spell. Samuel attacked one of the female ice demons. The female ice demon attacked with it's sharp pointed arms. Samuel defended with his small metal shield and then attacked with his sword killing the ice demon. Elrond fired a fireball spell killing the remaining female ice demon.

They searched the room and found a stone switch raised above the floor. Samuel tried to push down on it to activate it, but it didn't move. Samuel pushed down with his whole body weight, but it still didn't move. Above them in the air was a large square stone weight hanging above the switch in the air attached to the ceiling by a chain.

"Maybe that stone weight can be lowered to activate the switch", suggested Torell.

"But there is no leaver in the room", said Samuel.

"Let's see if there is a secret door hidden in this room that might lead to where the leaver is", suggested Torell.

They all started to search the room to see if they could find a secret door. They all found nothing.

"Maybe we missed a secret door on the way here", said John.

"Or maybe the leaver is on the other side of the east arch behind the portcullis", suggested Samuel.

"How then are we going to get pass the other portcullis?" John asked.

"John if you fire a blast from your fire sword it might melt the chain and cause the stone weight to fall. That way I can save my magic power", suggested Elrond.

John aimed his fire sword towards the chain and fired a fire blast. The chain got hot and then started to melt one of the links in the chain and the weight of the stone broke the chain, and the stone weight fell down onto the stone switch activating it. They could hear in the distance a chain raising. They returned to the main entrance and the portcullis to the east was raised.

They entered the east arch and entered a corridor. One female ice demon stood guard and fired ice shards at Samuel. Samuel defended with his shield. John fired a fire blast from his sword killing the ice demon. They entered a room with ice covering the floor. A long pit either side lined along the side of walls.

"Tread carefully. Try not to slip towards the pits", suggested Torell.

They started to cross the room slowly and Sarah started to slip towards one of the pits on the left.

"Sarah, hold out your spear so I can grab hold of you", suggested Samuel. Sarah did as Samuel suggested. "I got you!" Samuel said grabbing hold of Sarah's spear.

"Thanks, that was close", said Sarah.

They exited the room and came to a corridor. At the end of the corridor it went left and right. Torell checked for traps and found a trap to the right. They went left and came to another room. There was a table made of ice in the centre of the room. Elrond searched the table and found a rope on the table and took it. On the ground was a frozen body of a man. Torell searched the body and found a strange shaped knife with a wide shaped handle. Torell took the knife. They exited the room and came to a corridor that went left and right. Torell checked for traps and found a trap to the right. They went left and entered a small room. The room was empty. They searched for a secret door and found one. They entered another empty small room. They searched the room and Elrond found a switch and activated it. They returned to the corridor and a part of the wall had opened revealing a secret door. They entered through the secret door and went down a corridor until they came to a small room. In the centre of the room was a large icy pit. The floor was slippery because of ice.

"We are not all going to make it across here safely with out one of us falling down into that pit", said John.

"I have an idea. I will go across first using the rope Elrond found. Then when I am safe on the other side you can hold onto the rope and cross over one behind the other", suggested Torell.

"All right, let's try it", said Samuel.

Torell used the strange knife he found and tired one end to the rope to it. Torell stuck the knife into the icy covered wall. Torell then tired the other end of the rope to himself. Torell started to edge his way around the room. The others held the rope in case Torell fell. Torell made it halfway across the other side and he slipped on the icy floor. Torell fell over the side and the others pulled tight on the rope stopping Torell from falling any further. The others pulled back on the rope pulling Torell back. Torell grabbed back onto the side of the icy path and climbed back up. Torell continued to cross and made it to the other side. Each person crossed one after the other. Samuel held the rope from behind and he was the last to cross. Samuel took the knife out from the wall and tired the rope to himself. The others held onto the rope as he crossed. As Samuel started to cross he slipped. Samuel started to fall quite far. The others pulled tight on the rope breaking his fall. They pulled Samuel back and Samuel climbed back up. Samuel continued across and made it to the other side.

They continued down a corridor. A female ice demon attacked Sarah. Sarah killed it with her spear. The corridor turned to the left. They came to a small room with two more ice demons. There were also some stairs leading upwards and another exit door on the other side of the room. John killed one with a blast from his fire sword and Torell killed the other with an arrow fired from his bow.

They went up the stairs and entered a long hall with two blue knights that stood on guard by the entrance. The blue knights wore full metal armour that covered and protected their whole body.

"I wish Gillian was here to fight with us", said Sarah.

John fired a blast with his fire sword at one of the knights and the knight guarded the attack with his shield. Torell fired an arrow at the other knight and the knight used his shield to defend against the attack. Samuel and John fought with the knights with their swords. The knights defended well against their attacks and Samuel and John defended well against the knights attacks. Elrond used a freeze spell to freeze one of the knights and John finished the knight off with his sword. Samuel continued fighting and finally he killed the other knight.

They entered the next room with four crystal pillars supporting a high arched ceiling. The ice queen stood up from her throne and walked down some steps to their level.

"I promise you, you will not leave here alive. Ice demons kill them", said the ice queen.

Four female ice demons attacked. Torell killed one and Sarah killed another. One ice demon froze Elrond with a freeze spell. John fired his fire sword killing one. Torell used his anti-magic spell to release Elrond. Samuel defended against an ice shard blast from the remaining ice demon and finished her off with his sword. John aimed at the ice queen and fired a fire blast from his sword. The ice queen used a magic spell to cast a blue magic shield to protect herself. The ice queen fired a freeze spell at John freezing him on the spot. The ice queen then cast a shower of twenty ice shards towards them. Samuel took cover behind one of the crystal pillars. Sarah used her shield spell to protect the others. Torell took aim and fired an arrow. The arrow hit the ice queen's shield and then the arrow lay broken on the floor.

"Ha, ha, ha. You are no match for me. Your magic and weapons are useless against me", said the ice queen.

The ice queen cast a crystal pillar spell and ice shot up from the ground encasing Elrond, Samuel, and Sarah. Torell took cover behind one of the crystal pillars to avoid her spell. Torell fired an arrow at the ice queen. The arrow just bounced off the ice queen's blue shield and fell on the floor. The ice queen fired a freeze blast towards Torell. Torell took cover behind a crystal pillar protecting himself. Torell ran to where Elrond was trapped and cast an anti-magic spell to free him.

Elrond took out the sun amulet from under his cloak and held it up to the sky. The sun beamed against it and the light reflected back towards the ice queen. The green gem in its centre pieced the ice queen's blue shield and the light started to burn into her skin.

"It's not over yet", the ice queen screamed and started to cast her final spell. "Ceiling shards fall!"

She then fell to the floor smouldering away until she sudden burst into blue flames. All that remained on the floor was a silver key on a chain that she kept around her waist. With the ice queen dead her spell wore off and the others found themselves free from being trapped in crystal ice as it melted away onto the floor. Samuel walked up to where the ice queen had died and picked up the silver key.

"The demon lord was wise to have powerful demons guard these keys but we have four more to find and then our quest is almost over", said Samuel.

The others cheered. Ice shards started to break from the ceiling and started to fall. It was the ice queen's final spell that she had cast.

"Let's get out of here quick", said Samuel.

Samuel shielded his head with his small metal shield as ice shards fell and shattered around them. Ice fell and broke into pieces shattering on the cold icy floor spreading across the floor like broken glass.

"Be careful where you tread", warned Elrond.

More ice shards shattered on the floor as it fell from the ceiling, some shattered and ice splinters bounced off the floor and hit the side of Samuels leg. They exited the room and went down the stairs to the lower floor in the next room. They came to the pit room and quickly tied the rope across Torell so he could cross the room. Ice fell from the ceiling as he crossed. Once to the other side the others followed holding onto the rope while Torell held onto the other end. Samuel and John held their shields above their heads to protect themselves from falling ice from the ceiling. Once across they left the rope and exited the room as fast as they could.

They returned back to where Gillian and Alsta was by the main entrance and then they left the crystal palace. Sarah treated Samuel's, Elrond's, and Torell's wounds from the shards of ice which had cut them. Sarah healed Alsta's foot as best she could but it was too bad a wound to heal completely. Gillian carried Alsta over the snow back to the stone circle with the others. Elrond cast the teleportion spell and used the gnome stone to transport them all back to the stone circle near the elf woods. The gnome stone turned black after teleporting them all back to the stone circle near Elf Wood.

"Why has the stone turned black?" Samuel asked.

"All the magic has been used up teleporting us there, and back. The magic can only be used twice. To be able to use a stone circle to teleport again we will need to find another gnome stone", explained Elrond.

"What now Samuel?" John asked.

"I think we could all do with a rest. We have come this far and I think it is time to celebrate at our village Potters Den", answered Samuel.

"I will return to my people for the time being", said Torell.

"Can I go with you to Elf Castle until my foot gets better? And when it is better I will journey back to my people near the mountains", said Alsta.

"Yes, that will be fine. My people can take care of you until your foot is better and then I can escort you back to your village", said Torell.

"Thank you", said Alsta.

"Alsta, will you be able to continue with us on our quest when your foot is better?" Samuel asked.

"Yes, I live for adventure and it has been an honour for me to work with you", said Alsta.

"Will your people welcome you home because you left them?" Sarah asked.

"I will tell them of my many adventures that I have had with you. They will see that I have made them proud by fighting the evil in this land. If not I will join with you on your quest Samuel", replied Alsta.

"Farewell Torell and Alsta, and we will meet again in three months time to further our quest", said Samuel.

"Farewell." Torell and Alsta said.

"Farewell", they all replied.

They all said goodbye to Torell and Alsta as they went towards Torell's homeland.

They returned to their village the Potters Den and was gladly welcomed.

Roger had recovered from his injury and returned to Potters Den and was there to greet Samuel and the others as they entered Potters Den, "Good to see you all again."

"You too Roger", said Samuel. "How are you feeling?"

"I am a lot better now, ready for action to join you on another quest", said Roger.

"I am glad you are better and I am glad you still want to join us on our quest, but now it's time to celebrate", said Samuel.

They held a celebration for them all and talked about their adventures. Sarah joined in with the celebrations at Potters Den. Samuel did not tell the villagers of Potters Den the true reason for their quest and made it sound that they were adventures in search for lost or hidden treasure.

The reason for this was to try and prevent the true intent of their quest from reaching the demon lord who lived in demon castle among the black mountains. If news spread to the demon lord that they had already found three of the Seventh Tower keys, they could be hunted down and killed by armies of orcs.

They ate until they were full, and they sang, and drunk and told stories of their adventures until it was dark.